Anna Gavalda is one
writing in French. He
thirty languages and in
Waiting for Me Somewhere
Gathering and *Consolation*.

D0533447

Someone I Loved

Someone I Loved

Anna Gavalda

Translated from the French by Catherine Evans

Someone I Loved

Anna Gavalda

Translated from the French by Catherine Evans

Gallic Books
London

A Gallic Book

First published in France as *Je l'aimais* by Le Dilettante, 2002
English translation copyright © Penguin Group (USA) Inc., 2005
First published in the UK by Vintage as part of the collection, *I Wish Someone Were Waiting for me Somewhere*

Published by Gallic Books, 2012
Gallic Books, 59 Ebury Street, London, SW1W 0NZ
This edition published 2013

Every reasonable effort has been made to contact copyright holders and obtain the necessary permissions. In the event of an inadvertent omission or error please notify the editorial department at Gallic Books, at the address shown above, for the correction to be made in future printings.

A CIP record for this books is available from the British Library
ISBN 978-1-908313-48-5

Typeset in Fournier MT by Gallic Books
Printed and bound by CPI Group (UK) Ltd, Croydon, CR0 4YY

2 4 6 8 10 9 7 5 3 1

For Constance

'What did you say?'

'I said I'm going to take them. It will do them good to get away for a while.'

'But when?' my mother-in-law asked.

'Now.'

'Now? You're not thinking …'

'Yes, I am.'

'What are you talking about? It's nearly eleven! Pierre, you –'

'Suzanne, I'm talking to Chloé. Chloé, listen to me. I want to take you away from here. What do you say?'

I say nothing.

'Do you think it's a bad idea?'

'I don't know.'

'Go and get your things. We'll leave when you get back here.'

'I don't want to stop at my place first.'

'Then don't. We'll sort everything out when we're there.'

'But you don't –'

'Chloé, Chloé, please. Trust me.'

*

My mother-in-law continued to protest:

'But –! You're not really going to wake up the children! The house isn't even heated, and there's nothing to eat! Nothing for the girls! They –'

He stood up.

...

Marion is sleeping in her car seat, her thumb touching the edge of her lips. Lucie is beside her, rolled in a ball.

I look at my father-in-law. He sits upright. His hands grip the steering wheel. He hasn't said a word since we left. I see his profile in the headlights of oncoming cars. I think that he is as unhappy as I am. That he's tired. Disappointed.

He feels my gaze:

'Why don't you get some sleep? You should get some rest, you know – lean your seat back and go to sleep. We've got a long way to go …'

'I can't,' I tell him. 'I'm watching over you.'

He smiles at me. It's barely a smile.

'No … it's the other way around.'

We return to our private thoughts.
I cry behind my hands.

We're parked at a service station. I take advantage of his absence to check my mobile.

No messages.

Of course.

What a fool I am.

What a fool ...

I turn the radio on, then off.

He returns.

'Do you want to go in? Do you want something?'

I give in.

I press the wrong button; my cup fills with a nauseating liquid that I throw away at once.

In the store, I buy a pack of nappies for Lucie and a toothbrush for myself.

He refuses to start the car until I have leaned my seat back.

...

I opened my eyes as he switched off the engine.

'Don't move. Stay here with the girls while it's still warm. I'll go and turn on the radiators in your room. Then I'll come and get you.'

I pleaded with my phone.

At four in the morning …

I'm such a fool.

No way to go back to sleep.

The three of us are lying in Adrien's grandmother's bed, the one that creaks so horribly. It was our bed.

We would try to make love with as little movement as possible.

The whole house would hear if you moved an arm or a leg. I remember Christine's insinuations when we came down to breakfast the first morning. We blushed into our coffee and held hands under the table.

We learned our lesson. After that, we made love as quietly as anyone possibly could.

I know that he will return to this bed with someone else, and that with her, too, he will pick up this big mattress and throw it on the floor when they can't stand it any longer.

It's Marion who wakes us up. She is making her doll run along the quilt, and telling a story about flying lollipops. Lucie touches my eyelashes: 'Your eyes are all stuck together.'

We dress under the covers, because the room is too cold.

The creaking bed makes them laugh.

My father-in-law has lit a fire in the kitchen. I see him at the end of the garden, looking for logs in the woodshed.

This is the first time I've been alone with him.

I've never felt comfortable in his presence. Too distant. Too silent. And with everything Adrien told me about how hard it was growing up beneath his gaze, his harshness, his rages, the dramas about school.

It was the same with Suzanne. I never saw them be affectionate with each other. 'Pierre is not very demonstrative, but I know what he feels for me,' she told me one day when we were talking about love while snapping the ends off green beans.

14

I nodded, but I didn't understand. I didn't understand this man who minimised and controlled his passions. To show nothing for fear of appearing weak – I could never understand that. In my family, touching and kissing are like breathing.

I remember a stormy evening in this kitchen ... Christine, my sister-in-law, was complaining about her children's teachers, calling them incompetent and small-minded. From there, the conversation drifted into education in general, then hers in particular. And then the winds changed. Menacingly. The kitchen was transformed into a courtroom, with Adrien and his sister as the prosecutors, and in the dock – their father. It was horrible ... If only the lid had finally blown off, but no. All the bitterness was pushed down again, and they avoided a big explosion by making do with a few deadly jabs.

As usual.

What would have been possible, anyway? My father-in-law refused to take the bait. He listened to his children's bitter words without a word of response. 'Your criticisms roll off me like water off a duck's back,' he always said, smiling, before leaving the room.

This time, though, the argument had been fiercer.

I can still see his strained face, his hands gripping the water jug as though he had wanted to smash it before our eyes.

I imagined all those words that he would never say and I tried to understand. What possessed him? What did he think about when he was alone? And what was he like – intimately?

In despair, Christine turned to me:

'And you, Chloé, what do you make of all this?'

I was tired, I wanted the evening to be over. I had had it up to here with their family drama.

'Me?' I said thoughtfully. 'I think that Pierre doesn't live among us, I mean not really. He's a kind of Martian lost in the Dippel family …'

The others shrugged and turned away. But not him.

He loosened his grip on the jug. His face relaxed and he smiled at me. It was the first time I had ever seen him smile in that way. Maybe the last time, too. I think we developed some sort of understanding that evening … something subtle. I had tried to defend him as best I could, my odd, grey-haired Martian, who was now walking toward the kitchen door pushing a wheelbarrow full of wood.

…

'Is everything all right? You're not cold?'

'Yes, yes, everything's fine, thanks.'

'And the girls?'

'They're watching cartoons.'

'There are cartoons on at this hour?'

'They're on every morning during the school holidays.'

'Oh ... great. You found the coffee?'

'Yes, thanks.'

'And what about you, Chloé? Speaking of holidays, shouldn't you –'

'Call the office?'

'Well, I just thought –'

'Yes, yes, I'm going to do it, I ...'

I started to cry again.

My father-in-law lowered his gaze. He took off his gloves.

'I'm sorry, I'm interfering with something that's none of my business.'

'No, it's not that. It's just that ... I feel lost. I'm completely lost ... I ... you're right, I'll call my boss.'

'Who is your boss?'

'A friend. At least, I think she's a friend. We'll see ...'

I pulled my hair back with an old hairband of Lucie's that was in my pocket.

'Just tell her you're taking a few days off to take care of your cantankerous old father-in-law,' he suggested.

'All right ... I'll say cantankerous *and* impotent. That makes it sound more serious.'

He smiled as he blew on his cup of coffee.

Laure wasn't in. I mumbled a few words to her assistant, who had a call on another line.

I also called home. Punched in the answering machine code. Nothing important.

What did I expect?

And once again, the tears came. My father-in-law entered and quickly left.

Go on, I told myself, you need to have a good healthy cry. Dry your tears, squeeze out the sponge, wring out your big, sad body and turn the page. Think about something else. One foot in front of the other and start again.

That's what everyone keeps saying. Just think about something else. Life goes on. Think of your daughters. You can't just let yourself go. Get a grip.

Yes, I know, I know, but: I just can't.

What does 'to live' mean, anyway? What does it really mean?

My children, what do I have to offer them? A messed-up mother? An upside-down world?

I really do want to get up in the morning, get dressed, feed myself, dress them, feed them, hang on until evening and then put them to bed and kiss them good night. I've done that, anybody can. But not any more.

For God's sake.

Not any more.

'Mum!'

'Yes?' I answered, wiping my nose on my sleeve.

'Mum!'

'I'm here, I'm here …'

Lucie stood in front of me, wearing her coat over her nightdress. She was swinging her Barbie doll around by the hair.

'You know what Grandpa said?'

'No.'

'He said we're going to go eat at McDonald's.'

'I don't believe you,' I answered.

'But it's true! He told us himself.'

'When?'

'A little while ago.'

'I thought he hated McDonald's …'

'Nope, he doesn't hate it. He said we're going shopping, and afterwards we're going to McDonald's – even you, even Marion, even me, and even him!'

She took my hand as we climbed the stairs.

'I don't have many clothes here, you know. We forgot them all in Paris.'

'That's true,' I said. 'We forgot everything.'

'And you know what Grandpa said?'

'No.'

'He told me and Marion that he's going to buy us clothes when we go shopping. And we can choose them ourselves.'

'Oh, really?'

I changed Marion's nappy, tickling her tummy as I did so.

All this time, Lucie sat on the edge of the bed and kept on talking.

'And then he said okay …'

'Okay to what?'

'To everything I asked for …'

Oh no …

'What did you ask for?'

'Barbie clothes.'

'For your Barbie?'

'For my Barbie and for me. The same for both!'

'Not those horrendous sparkly T-shirts?'

'Yes, and everything that goes with them: pink jeans, pink sneakers with Barbie on them, and socks with the little bow … You know … right there … the little bow at the back …'

She pointed at her ankle.

I laid Marion down.

'Beeeeoooootiful,' I told her, 'you're going to look just beeeeooooootiful!'

Her mouth twisted.

'Anyway, you think everything that's nice is *ugly*.'

I laughed; I kissed her adorable little frown.

She put on her dress, dreaming all the while.

*

'I'm going to look beautiful, huh?'

'You're already beautiful, my sweet. You're already very, very beautiful.'

'Yes, but even more ...'

'You think that's possible?'

She thought for a second.

'Yes, I think so.'

'Come on, turn around.'

What a wonderful invention little girls are, I thought as I combed her hair. What a wonderful invention.

As we queued at the checkout, my father-in-law admitted he hadn't set foot in a supermarket in more than ten years.

I thought about Suzanne.

Always alone, behind her shopping trolley.

Always alone everywhere.

After their chicken nuggets, the girls played in a sort of cage filled with coloured balls. A young man told them to take off their shoes, and I kept Lucie's awful 'You're a Barbie girl!' sneakers on my lap.

The worst thing was that they had a sort of transparent wedge heel …

'How could you have bought such hideous things?'

'It made her so happy … I'm trying not to make the same mistakes with the next generation. You see, it's like this place … Even if it had been possible, I would never have brought Christine and Adrien here thirty years ago. Never! And why, I ask myself now – why would I have deprived them of this type of pleasure? In the end, what would it have cost me? A miserable fifteen minutes? What's a miserable fifteen minutes compared with the shining faces of your kids?'

'I've done everything wrong,' he said, shaking his head. 'Even this bloody sandwich, I'm holding it the wrong way up, aren't I?'

His trousers were covered with mayonnaise.

'Chloé?'

'Yes.'

'I want you to eat. I'm sorry I'm talking to you as if you were Suzanne, but you haven't eaten anything since yesterday.'

'I can't seem to do it.'

He backed off.

'You're right – how could you eat something like this, anyway? Who could? Nobody!'

I tried to smile.

'All right, you can stay on a diet for now, but tonight, it's over! Tonight I'm making dinner, and you're going to have to make an effort, all right?'

'All right.'

'And this? How do you eat this astronaut thing, anyway?'

He held up an improbable salad sealed in a plastic shaker.

...

We spent the rest of the afternoon in the garden. The girls fluttered around their grandfather, who had got it into his head to mend the old swing. I watched them from a distance, sitting on the steps. It was cold but clear. The sun shone in their hair, and I thought they were lovely.

I thought about Adrien. What was he doing?

Where was he at this exact moment?

And with whom?

And our life, what was it going to look like?

Every thought drew me closer to the bottom. I was so tired. I shut my eyes. I dreamed that he had arrived. There was the sound of an engine in the courtyard, he sat down next to me, he kissed me and put his finger to my lips in order to surprise the girls. I can still feel his tender touch on my neck, his voice, his warmth, the smell of his skin, it's all there.

It's all there ...

All I have to do is think about it.

How long does it take to forget the smell of someone who loved you? How long until you stop loving?

If only someone would give me an hourglass.

...

The last time we were in each other's arms, I was the one who kissed him. It was in the lift in the Rue de Flandre.

He didn't resist.

Why? Why did he let himself be kissed by a woman he no longer loved? Why did he give me his lips? His arms?

It doesn't make any sense.

The swing is fixed. Pierre shoots me a glance. I turn my head. I don't want to meet his gaze. I'm cold, my nose is running, and I have to go and heat the bathroom.

'What can I do to help?'

He had tied a dish towel around his waist.

'Lucie and Marion are in bed?'

'Yes.'

'They won't be cold?'

'No, no, they're fine. Tell me what I can do.'

'You can cry without embarrassing me for once … It would do me good to see you cry for no reason. Here, cut these up,' he added, handing me three onions.

'You think I cry too much?'

'Yes.'

Silence.

I picked up the wooden cutting board near the sink and sat down across from him. His face was tight once again. The only sounds came from the fireplace.

•••

'That's not what I meant to say …'

'I'm sorry?'

'I didn't mean to say that. I don't think you cry too much,

I'm just overwhelmed. You're so pretty when you smile …'

'Would you like a drink?'
  I nodded.

'Let's let it warm up a bit, it would be a shame otherwise …
Do you want a Bushmills while we're waiting?'
  'No, thanks.'
  'Why not?'
  'I don't like whisky.'
  'What a shame! This isn't just whisky. Here, taste this.'
  I put the glass to my lips; it tasted like lighter fluid. I
hadn't eaten for days, and suddenly I was drunk. My knife
slipped on the onion skins, and my head rolled on my neck.
I thought I was going to chop off a finger. I felt just fine.

'It's good, isn't it? Patrick Frendall gave it to me for my
sixtieth birthday. Do you remember Patrick Frendall?'
  'Uh … no.'
  'Yes, you do. You met him here, don't you remember?
A big fellow with huge arms.'
  'The one who tossed Lucie in the air until she was about
to throw up?'
  'That's the one,' Pierre said, pouring me another drink.
  'Yes, I remember.'
  'I really like him; I think about him a lot. It's odd, I
consider him to be one of my best friends and I hardly
know him.'

'Do you have best friends?'

'Why do you ask that?'

'Just to ask, I … I don't know. I've never heard you talk about them.'

My father-in-law threw himself into cutting carrot rounds. It's always amusing to watch a man cook for the first time in his life. That way of following a recipe to the letter, as if Delia Smith were looking over his shoulder.

'It says "cut the carrots in medium-sized rounds". Do you think these will do like this?'

'Perfect!'

I laughed. With a rubber neck, my head lolled on my shoulders.

'Thanks. So, where was I? Oh yes, my friends … I've had three in my life. I met Patrick on a trip to Rome, some sort of pious nonsense organised by the local church. My first trip without my parents … I was fifteen. I didn't understand a word this Irishman, twice my size, was saying to me, but we got along immediately. He had been brought up in the most Catholic family in the world, and I was just getting out from under my suffocating family … Two young hounds unleashed in the Eternal City … What a pilgrimage that was!'

It still gave him a thrill.

He heated the onions and carrots in a casserole with bits of smoked ham. It smelled wonderful.

'And then there's Jean Théron, whom you know, and my brother, Paul, who you never met because he died in '56.'

'You considered your brother to be your best friend?'

'He was even more than that. Chloé, from what I know of you, you would have adored him. He was sensitive, funny, attentive to everyone, always in a good mood. He painted ... I'll show you his watercolours tomorrow, they're in my study. He knew all the bird calls. He liked to tease people, but never harmed a soul. He was charming, really charming. Everyone loved him ...'

'What did he die of?'

My father-in-law turned away.

'He went to Indochina. He came back sick and half-mad. He died of tuberculosis on Bastille Day, 1956.'

I said nothing.

'I don't need to tell you that after that, my parents never watched a single parade again for the rest of their lives. Celebrations, fireworks, that was the end of that.'

He added pieces of meat and turned them over, browning them on all sides.

'You see, the worst part was that he had volunteered. He was still at school at the time. He was dazzling. He wanted to work at the National Forestry Office. He loved trees and birds. He should never have gone over there. He had no reason to go. None. He was gentle, a pacifist. He quoted Giono, and he –'

'So why did he go?'

'Because of a girl. Your typical unhappy love affair. It was ridiculous; she wasn't even a woman, just a young girl. It was absurd. Even as I'm telling you this – and every time I think about it – I'm just floored by the inanity of our lives. A good boy goes off to war because of a sulky young lady … it's grotesque. It's something you read in bad novels. It's like a soap opera, a story like that.'

'She didn't love him?'

'No. But Paul was crazy about her. He adored her. He had known her since she was twelve; he wrote her letters she probably didn't even understand. He went swaggering off to war. So she could see what a man he was! And the night before he left, the ass, he told everyone: "When she asks you, don't give her my address right away. I want to be the first to write." Three months later, she got engaged to the son of the butcher on the Rue de Passy.'

He shook a dozen different spices into the pot, whatever he could find in the cupboards.

I shuddered to think what Delia would have said.

'A big pale boy who spent his days boning cuts of meat in the back of his father's shop. You can imagine what a shock it was for us. She ditched our Paul for this big lump. He was over there, halfway around the world, he was probably thinking about her, writing poetry for her, the fool, and she, all she could think about was going out

30

with an oaf who was allowed to borrow his father's car on Saturday night. A sky-blue Renault Frégate, as I recall … Of course, she was free not to love him, but Paul was too impetuous, he never could do anything without bravura, without … without flair. What a waste …'

'And then?'

'And then nothing. Paul came home and my mother switched butchers. He spent a lot of time in this house, which he hardly ever left. He drew, read, complained that he couldn't sleep. He suffered a great deal, coughed constantly, and then he died. At twenty- one.'

'You've never spoken of him.'

'No.'

'Why?'

'I always liked talking about him with people who had known him; it was easier …'

I pushed my chair back from the table.

'I'll set the table. Where do you want to eat?'

'Here in the kitchen is fine.'

He switched off the overhead light, and we sat down, facing each other.

'It's delicious.'

'Do you really think so? It seems a bit overcooked, don't you think?'

'No, no, really, it's perfect.'

'You're too good.'

'It's your wine that's good. Tell me about Rome.'

'About the city?'

'No, about this pilgrimage ... What were you like when you were fifteen?'

'Oh ... what was I like? I was the stupidest boy in the world. I tried to keep up with Frendall's big strides. I talked incessantly, told him about Paris, the Moulin Rouge, said anything that came into my head, and lied shamelessly. He laughed and said things that I didn't understand either, which made me laugh in turn. We spent our time stealing coins from the fountains and smirked every time we met someone of the opposite sex. We were completely pathetic, when I think of it now. I don't remember the goal of the pilgrimage any more. There was no doubt a good cause, an occasion for prayer, as they say. I don't remember any more. For me, it was a huge breath of fresh air. Those few days changed my life. I discovered the taste of freedom. It was like ... would you like some more?'

'Yes, please.'

'You have to understand the context. We were all pretending we had just won a war. There was so much ill-will in the air. We couldn't mention anyone's name, a neighbour, a shopkeeper, a friend's parents, without my father immediately pigeonholing them – this one's an informer, that one was denounced, a coward, a good-for-nothing. It was horrible. It's perhaps hard to imagine it now, but believe me, it was horrible for us children. We hardly spoke to him, or very little. Probably just the strict minimum. But one day, I asked him, "If you think humanity is so awful, then why did you go and fight for it?" '

'What did he answer?'

'Nothing … just dismissed it.'

'Stop, stop, that's plenty!'

'I was living on the second floor of a building that was completely grey, buried in the sixteenth arrondissement. It was such a sad … My parents couldn't afford to live there, but the address was prestigious, you see. The sixteenth! We were squeezed into a grim apartment that never got any sun, and where my mother forbade us to open the windows because there was a bus depot just underneath. She was mortally afraid that the curtains would … would become soiled … oh, this nice little Bordeaux has me speaking like her … I was terribly bored. I was too young to interest my father and my mother just fluttered around.

'She went out a lot. "Time spent helping in the parish," she would say, rolling her eyes. She overdid it, acted shocked at the behaviour of certain church ladies whom she had made up out of thin air. She would take off her gloves and toss them on the hall table as if she were throwing in her notice, then sigh, prance around, chatter, lie, sometimes tripping herself up. We just let her talk. Paul called her Sarah Bernhardt, and after she left the room my father would resume reading *Le Figaro* without a word … Some potatoes?'

'No, thanks.'

'I was a half-boarder at the Lycée Janson-de-Sailly. I was as grey as my building. I read Catholic comics and the adventures of Flash Gordon. I played tennis with the Mortellier boys every Thursday. I … I was a very good, very dull boy. I dreamed of taking the lift to the sixth floor just to have a look … Talk about an adventure! Going up to the sixth floor! I was soft in the head, I swear.

'I was waiting for Patrick Frendall.

'I was waiting for the Pope!'

He got up to stoke the fire.

'Anyway, the trip wasn't a revolution … a bit of a lark at most. I always thought I would … how shall I say … throw off the yoke one day. But no. Never. I kept on being that very good, very dull boy. But why am I telling you all this? Why am I so talkative all of a sudden?'

'It was me that asked the question.'

'Well, that's still no reason! I'm not boring you to death with my trip down memory lane?'

'No, no, on the contrary. I really like it.'

...

The following morning, I found a note on the kitchen table: *Gone to office. Back later.*

There was hot coffee, and an enormous log on the fire.

34

Why didn't he tell me he was going?

What a strange man … Like a fish, always twisting away from you, slipping out of your hands.

I poured myself a large cup of coffee and drank it standing up, leaning against the kitchen window. I looked at the robins swarming around the block of lard that the girls had put out on the bench the previous day.

The sun had almost risen above the hedge.

I was waiting for them to wake up. The house was too quiet.

I wanted a cigarette. It was stupid, I hadn't smoked in years. But that's what life is like … You show what incredible willpower you have, and then one winter morning you decide to walk four kilometres in the cold to buy a pack of cigarettes. You love a man, you have two children with him, and one winter morning, you learn that he has left because he loves someone else. Adding that he doesn't know what to say, that he made a mistake.

Like calling a wrong number: 'I'm sorry, it was a mistake.'

Why, think nothing of it …

Like a soap bubble.

It's windy. I go out to put the lard out of the way.

I watch television with the girls. I'm horrified: the

characters in the cartoons seem so stupid and spoiled. Lucie gets annoyed, shakes her head, begs me to be quiet. I want to tell her about Candy.

When I was little, I was hooked on Candy.

Candy never talked about money, only about love. And then I shut up. That will teach me to act like little miss Candy ...

The wind blows harder and harder. I give up the idea of walking to the village.

We spend the afternoon in the attic. The girls play dressing-up. Lucie waves a fan in her sister's face:

'Are you too hot, Countess?'

The Countess can't move. She has too many hats on her head.

We bring down an old cradle. Lucie says that it needs a new coat of paint.

'Pink?' I ask her.

'How did you guess?'

'I'm very clever.'

The telephone rings. Lucie answers.

At the end, I hear her ask:

'Do you want to talk to Mummy now?'

She hangs up shortly after. Doesn't come back and join us.

I continue to strip the cradle with Marion.

I find her when I go down to the kitchen, her chin on the table. I sit down next to her.

We look at each other.

'One day, will you and Papa be in love again?'

'No.'

'Are you sure?'

'Yes.'

'I already knew it, anyway …'

She got up and added:

'You know what else?'

'No, what?'

'The birds have already eaten everything …'

'Really? Are you sure?'

'Yes, come see.'

She came around the table and took my hand.

We were in front of the window. There was my little blonde girl next to me. She was wearing an old dress-shirt and a moth-eaten skirt. Her 'You're a Barbie girl!' sneakers fitted right into her great-grandmother's button-up shoes. Her mother's large hand fitted completely around hers. We watched the trees in the garden bending in the wind, and probably thought the same thing …

The bathroom was so cold that I couldn't lift my shoulders out of the water. Lucie shampooed our hair and gave us all sorts of wild hairdos. 'Look, Mum! You've got horns on your head!'

I knew it already.

It wasn't very funny, but it made me laugh.

'Why are you laughing?'

'Because I'm stupid.'

'Why are you stupid?'

We danced about to dry ourselves off.

Nightdresses, socks, shoes, sweaters, dressing gowns, and more sweaters.

My two little Michelin men went down to have their soup.

There was a power cut just as Babar was playing with the lift in a big department store, under the angry gaze of the operator. Marion started to cry.

'Wait here, I'll go and turn the lights back on.'

'Waah! Waaaaahhhh!'

'Stop that, Barbie Girl, you've made your sister cry.'

'Don't call me Barbie Girl!'

'So stop.'

It wasn't the circuit breaker or a fuse. The shutters banged, the doors creaked, and the whole house was plunged into darkness.

Brontë sisters, pray for us.

I wondered when Pierre was going to return.

I brought the girls' mattress down into the kitchen. Without an electric radiator, it was impossible to let them sleep up there. They were as excited as could be. We pushed back the table and laid their makeshift bed next to the fireplace.

I lay down between them.

'And Babar? You didn't finish …'

'Hush, Marion, hush. Look right in front of you. Look at the fire. That's what will tell you stories …'

'Yes, but …'

'Shhhh.'

They fell asleep immediately.

...

I listened to the sounds of the house. My nose itched, and I rubbed my eyes to keep from crying.

My life is like this bed, I kept thinking. Fragile. Uncertain. Suspended.

I lay there waiting for the house to blow away.

*

I was thinking that I had been cast off.

It's funny how expressions are not just expressions. You have to have experienced real fear to understand the meaning of 'cold sweat', or been very anxious to know exactly what 'my stomach was in knots' means, right?

It's the same with 'cast off '. What a marvellous expression. I wonder who thought it up.

Cast off the mooring lines.

Untie the wife.

Take to the sea, spread your albatross wings, and go and fuck on some other horizon.

No, really, what better way to put it?

I'm starting to sound bitter; that's a good sign. Another few weeks and I'll be really nasty.

The trap really lies in thinking that you are moored. You make decisions, take out loans, sign agreements, and even take a few risks. You buy houses, put the children in rooms all painted pink, and sleep entwined every night. You marvel at this … What is it called? This *intimacy*. Yes, that's what it was called, when you were happy. And even when you were less happy …

The trap lies in thinking that we have the right to be happy.

How ridiculous we are. Naïve enough to think that for even a second we have control over our lives.

Our lives slip through our fingers, but it's not serious. It's not that important …

The best thing would be to know it earlier.
When exactly 'earlier'?
Earlier.
Before repainting the bedrooms in pink, for example …
Pierre is right, why show your weakness?
Just to be hurt?

My grandmother often said that nice home cooking was the best way to keep a good man. I'm certainly a long way off, Grandma, a long way. First, I don't know how to cook, and then, I never wanted to keep anyone.

Well, then, you've succeeded, Granddaughter!
I pour myself a little cognac to celebrate.

One little tear and then bedtime.

The following day seemed very long.

We went for a walk. We gave bread to the horses at the riding school and spent a lot of time with them. Marion sat on the back of a pony. Lucie didn't want to.

I felt as if I were carrying a very heavy backpack.

In the evening it was showtime. Lucky me – every night there's a show at my house. On this evening's programme: 'The Little Gurl Who Dident Wanta Leev'. They took great pains to distract me.

I didn't sleep well.

The next morning, my heart wasn't in it. It was too cold.

...

The girls whined endlessly.

I tried to amuse them by pretending to be a prehistoric cavewoman.

'Now look, this is how the cavemen used to make their Nesquik … They put a pan of milk on the fire, yes, just like that … and to make toast? Simple as can be, they put a piece of bread on a grill and voilà, they held it over the flames … Careful! Not too long, or it will burn to a crisp. Okay, who wants to play cavewoman with me?'

They didn't care, they weren't hungry. All they cared about was their stupid television shows.

I burned myself. Marion started to cry when she heard me yell, and Lucie spilled her cocoa on the couch.

I sat down and put my head in my hands.

I dreamed of being able to unscrew my head, put it on the ground in front of me, and kick it hard enough to send it flying as far as possible.

So far that no one would ever find it again.

But I don't even know how to kick.

I wouldn't shoot straight, that's for sure.

At that moment, Pierre arrived.

He was sorry, explained that he couldn't get in touch earlier because the line was down, and shook a bag of warm croissants under the girls' noses.

They laughed. Marion took his hand and Lucie offered him a prehistoric coffee.

'A prehistoric coffee? With pleasure, my little Cro-Magnon beauty!'

I had tears in my eyes.

He placed a hand on my knee.

'Chloé … Are you all right?'

I wanted to tell him no, that I was not in the least bit all right, but I was so happy to see him that I answered the opposite.

'The bakery has lights, so it's not a local power cut. I'll go and find out what's happened … Girls, look outside, the weather is beautiful! Go and get dressed – we're going mushroom hunting. With all the rain last night, we're going to find plenty!'

The 'girls' included me … We climbed the stairs giggling.

How nice to be eight years old.

We walked all the way to the Devil's Mill, a sinister old building that has delighted several generations of small children.

Pierre told the girls stories about the holes in the walls:

'Here's where his horn struck … and there, those are the marks of his hooves …'

'Why did he kick the wall with his hooves?'

'Oh, that's a long story … It was because he was very cross that day.'

'Why was he very cross that day?'

'Because his prisoner had escaped.'

'Who was his prisoner?'

'The girl at the bakery.'

'Madame Pécaut's daughter?'

'No, no, not her daughter! Her great-great-grandmother!'

'Really?'

I showed the girls how to have a miniature tea party with acorn caps. We found an empty bird's nest, pebbles, and pine cones. We picked cowslips and broke hazelnut branches. Lucie brought back moss for her dolls and Marion stayed on her grandfather's shoulders the whole time.

We brought back two mushrooms, both of them looked suspect!

On the way back, we heard a blackbird singing, and a little girl asking in a curious voice:

'But why did the devil capture Madame Pécaut's grandmother?'

'Can't you guess?'

'No.'

'Because he was very greedy, that's why!'

She thrashed at the underbrush with a stick to chase away the devil.

And what about me? I thought. What can I chase away with a stick?

...

'Chloé?'

'Yes.'

'I want to tell you … I hope … Or rather, I'd like … Yes, that's it, I'd like … I'd like you to feel you're still welcome at the house because … I know how much you love it. You've done so many things here. In the bedrooms, the garden … Until you came, there was no garden, you know? Promise me that you'll come back. With or without the girls …'

I turned towards him.

'No, Pierre. You know very well that I can't.'

'What about your rosebush? What is it called, anyway? That rosebush you planted last year?'

'Maiden's Blush.'

'Yes, that's it. You loved it so …'

'No, it's the name I loved. Listen, this is hard enough as it is …'

'I'm sorry, I'm sorry.'

'What about you? Can't you look after it?'

'Of course! Maiden's Blush, you say … How could I not?'

He was overdoing it a little.

On the way back, we ran into old Marcel, who was returning from the village. His bicycle was weaving dangerously across the road. How he managed to stop in front of us without falling off, I'll never know. He put Lucie on the seat and invited us for a quick drink.

46

*

Madame Marcel smothered the girls with kisses and planted them in front of the television with a bag of sweets on their knees. 'Mummy, she has a satellite dish! Guess what! A channel with nothing but cartoons!'

Thank God.

Go to the ends of the earth, clamber over thickets, hedges, ditches, get a stuffy nose, cross old Marcel's courtyard, and watch Teletoons while eating strawberry-flavoured marshmallows.

Sometimes, life is wonderful ...

The storm, mad cow disease, Europe, hunting, the dead and the dying ... At one point in the discussion, Pierre asked:

'Marcel, tell me, do you remember my brother?'

'Who, Paul? I should say I do, that little monkey ... He drove me crazy with that little whistling of his. Made me think there were all kinds of things to hunt! Made me think there were birds we don't have in these parts! That little rascal! And the dogs went crazy! Oh, I remember him all right! Such a great kid ... He often headed off into the forest with the priest. He wanted to see and know about everything ... My word, the questions that boy would ask! He always said he wanted to study so he could work in the forest. I remember how the priest would answer, "But, my boy, you don't need to go to school! What could you learn that I couldn't teach you?" Paul didn't answer, he said he wanted to visit all the forests in the world, to see other countries, travel through Africa and Russia, and then come back here and tell us all about it.'

Pierre listened to him, gently nodding his head to encourage the old man to keep talking.

Madame Marcel stood up. She returned and held out a sketchbook to us.

'Here's what little Paul – well, I call him little Paul, but he wasn't so little at the time – gave me one day to thank me for my special deep-fried acacia flowers. Look, that was my dog.'

As she turned the pages, you could see the tricks of a little fox terrier who looked spoiled to death and a real show-off.

'What was his name?' I asked.

'He didn't have a name, but we always called him Where'd-He-Go, because he was always running off. That's how he died, actually … Oh … We just loved that dog … We just loved him … Too much, too much. This is the first time I've looked at these drawings in a long time. Normally, I try not to poke around in here, it's too many deaths at once …'

The drawings were marvellous. Where'd-He-Go was a brown fox terrier with long black whiskers and bushy eyebrows.

'He was shot … He was poaching from poachers, the little imbecile …'

*

I got up. We had to leave before it got completely dark.

...

'My brother died because of the rain. Because he was stationed out in the rain too long, can you imagine?'

I didn't answer; I was too busy watching my step, trying to avoid the puddles.

The girls went to bed without supper. Too many sweets.

Babar left the Old Lady. She was alone. She cried. She asked herself, 'When will I see my little Babar again?'

Pierre was also unhappy. He stayed in his study a long time, supposedly looking for his brother's drawings. I made dinner. Spaghetti with bits of Suzanne's home-made *gésiers confits*.

We had decided to leave the next day before noon. This was going to be the last time I would cook in this kitchen.

I really loved this kitchen. I threw the pasta into boiling water, cursing myself for being so sentimental. *I really loved this kitche*n … Hey, get a grip, old girl, you'll find other kitchens …

I bullied myself, even though my eyes were filled with tears. It was stupid.

He put a small watercolour on the table. A woman, reading, seen from behind.

She was sitting on a garden bench. Her head was

slightly tilted. Perhaps she wasn't reading. Perhaps she was sleeping or daydreaming.

I recognised the house. The front steps, the rounded shutters, and the white wisteria.

'It's my mother.'

'What was her name?'

'Alice.'

I said nothing.

'It's for you.'

I started to protest, but he made an angry face and put a finger to his lips. Pierre Dippel was someone who didn't like to be contradicted.

'You always have to be obeyed, don't you?'

He wasn't listening to me.

'Didn't anyone ever dare to contradict you?' I added, placing Paul's drawing on the mantelpiece.

'Not one person. My entire life.'

I burned my tongue.

...

He pushed himself up from the table.

'Bah. What would you like to drink, Chloé?'

'Something that cheers you up.'

...

He came back up from the cellar, cradling two bottles as if they were newborn babies.

'Château Chasse-Spleen … appropriately enough. Just exactly what we need. I took two, one for you and one for me.'

'But you're crazy! You should wait for a better occasion … '

'A better occasion than what?'

He pulled his chair closer to the fire.

'Than … I don't know … than me … than us … than tonight.'

He had his arms wrapped around himself to keep his spirits up.

'But, Chloé, we're a great occasion. We're the best occasion in the world. I've been coming to this house since I was a boy, I've eaten thousands of meals in this kitchen, and, believe me, I know a great occasion when I see one!'

There was a little self-important tone in his voice. What a shame.

...

He turned his back and stared at the fire, motionless.

'Chloé, I don't want you to go …'

I tossed the noodles into the strainer and a dish towel on top.

'Look, I'm sorry, but this is too much. You're talking nonsense. You're only thinking about yourself, and it's a bit tiresome. "I don't want you to go." How can you say something so stupid? It wasn't me who left, okay? You have a son, remember him? Well, he was the one who left. It was him, didn't you know? It's a good story. It goes like this – it's a killer. So, it was … When was it, anyway? Doesn't matter. The other day, Adrien, the wonderful Adrien, packed his bags. Try and put yourself in my place – I was shocked. Oh right, I forgot to mention, it turns out I'm this boy's wife. You know, a wife, that practical thing you drag around everywhere, and that smiles when you kiss it. So, I was a bit surprised, as you can imagine … there he was with our suitcases standing in front of the lift, already groaning, looking at his watch. He was complaining because he was stressed out, the poor dear! The lift, the suitcases, the missus, and the plane, what a dilemma! Oh, yes! It seems he couldn't miss his plane because his mistress was on board! You know, a mistress, that young impatient thing that gets on your nerves a little. No time for a scene, you're thinking … And then, domestic quarrels are so tiresome … You never learn that at the Dippels', do you? Yelling, making scenes, moodiness, all so vulgar, don't you think? That's it, vulgar. With the Dippels, it's "never complain, never explain", and then on to the next thing. Now that's class.'

'Chloé, stop that at once!'

I was crying.

'Don't you hear yourself? Do you hear the way you talk to me? I'm not a dog, Pierre. I'm not your goddamned dog! I let him leave without ripping his eyes out, I quietly shut the door, and now I'm here, in front of you, in front of my children. I'm holding on. I'm just about holding on, do you understand? Do you understand what that means? Who heard me howl in despair? Who? So don't try to make me feel sorry for you now with your little problems. You don't want me to go … Oh, Pierre … I am unfortunately obliged to disobey you … It's with great regret … It's …'

He had grabbed hold of my wrists and was squeezing them as hard as he could. He held my arms immobile.

'Let me go! You're hurting me! This entire family is hurting me! Pierre, let me go.'

He barely had time to loosen his grip before my head fell on his shoulder.

'You're all hurting me …'

...

I cried into his neck, forgetting how uncomfortable it must have made him. Pierre, who never touched anyone. I cried, thinking occasionally about how the spaghetti was going to be inedible if I didn't add some oil. He said, 'Now, now …' He said, 'Please forgive me.' And he said, 'I'm just as sad as you …' He didn't know what to do with his hands any more.

Finally, he moved aside to lay the table.

'To you, Chloé.'

I clinked my glass against his.

'Yes, to me,' I repeated with a crooked smile.

'You're a wonderful girl.'

'Yes, wonderful. And then there's dependable, courageous … What did I leave out?'

'Funny.'

'Oh, right, I was forgetting. Funny.'

'But unfair.'

I said nothing.

'You are being a bit unfair, don't you think?'

Silence.

'You think that I only love myself?'

'Yes.'

'Well, then, you're not only unfair, you're being stupid.'

I held out my glass.

'Oh, that, I knew that already … Pour me some more of that marvellous nectar.'

'You think that I'm an old bastard, don't you?'

'Yes.'

I nodded my head. I wasn't being mean, I was unhappy. He sighed.

'Why am I an old bastard?'

'Because you don't love anyone. You never let yourself go. You're never there, never really with us. Never joining in our conversations and foolishness, never participating in dull dinner-table talk. Because you're never tender, because you never talk, and because your silence looks like disdain. Because –'

'Stop, stop. That will do, thanks.'

'Excuse me, I was answering your question. You ask me why you're an old bastard, and I'm telling you. That being said, you're not as old as all that ...'

'You're too kind.'

'Don't mention it.'

I grinned at him tenderly, baring my teeth.

'But if I'm the way you describe, why would I bring you here? Why would I spend so much time with you, and –'

'You know very well why.'

'Why?'

'Because of your sense of honour. That high-mindedness of good families. For seven years I've tagged along after you, and this is the first time you've taken any notice of me. I'll tell you what I think. I don't find you either benevolent or charitable. I can see exactly what's going on. Your son has done something stupid and you – you come along behind, you clean up and repair the damage. You're going to plaster over the cracks as best you can. Because you don't like cracks, do you, Pierre? Oh, no! You don't like them one bit ...

'Let me tell you something. I think you brought me here for the sake of appearances. The boy has messed up, well, let's grit our teeth and sort things out without making a fuss. In the past, you'd buy off the locals when the little shit's sports car made a mess of their beet fields, and today you're distracting the daughter-in-law. I'm just waiting for the moment when you put on your sorrowful act to tell me that I can count on you. Financially, I mean. *You're in a bit of a difficult spot, aren't you?* But a big girl like me is harder to buy off than a field of beets ...'

He got up. 'So yes ... It's true. You are stupid. What a terrible thing to discover ... Here, give me your plate.'

He was behind my back.

'You can't imagine how much that hurts. More than that, you've wounded me deeply. But I don't hold it against you – I blame it on the pain you are feeling ...'

He set a steaming plate in front of me.

'But there is one thing you can't get away with saying, just one thing ...'

'What's that?' I asked, lifting my gaze.

'Whatever you do, don't drag beets into this. You'd be hard-pressed to find a single beet field for miles around ...'

He was smugly pleased with himself.

'Mmm, this is good … You're going to miss my cooking, aren't you?'

'Your cooking, yes. As for the rest, thanks but no thanks … You've taken away my appetite …'

'Really?'

'No.'

'You had me worried there!'

'It would take more than that to keep me away from this marvellous pasta …'

He dug into his plate and lifted up a forkful of sticky spaghetti.

'Mmm, what do they call this? *Al dente* …'

I laughed.

'I love it when you laugh.'

…

For a long moment we didn't speak.

'Are you angry?'

'No, not angry. Confused, really …'

'I'm sorry.'

'You see, I feel as if I'm facing something impenetrable. A sort of enormous knot …'

'I'd like –'

'Hold on, hold on. Let me speak. I have to sort it

out now, it's very important. I don't know if you'll understand, but you must listen to me. I need to follow a thread, but which one? I don't know, I don't know how or where to begin. Oh God, it's so complicated … If I choose the wrong thread or pull too hard, it might tighten the knot even more. It might become so badly knotted that nothing could be done, and I'll leave you overwhelmed. You see, Chloé, my life, my whole life is like this closed fist. Here I am before you in this kitchen. I'm sixty-five years old. I'm not much to look at. I'm just an old bastard you were shaking a while ago. I have understood nothing, and I never went up to the sixth floor. I was afraid of my own shadow, and here I am, facing the idea of my own death and … No, please, don't interrupt me … Not now. Let me open this fist. Just a little bit.'

I refilled our glasses.

'I'll start with what's most unfair, most cruel … That is, with you …'

He let himself fall back against the back of his chair.

···

'The first time I saw you, you were completely blue. I remember how impressed I was. I can still see you standing in that doorway … Adrien was holding you up, and you held out a hand that was completely stiff with cold. You couldn't greet me, you couldn't speak, so I squeezed your arm in a sign of welcome, and I can still see the white marks that my fingers left on your wrist. Suzanne was panicking, but Adrien told her, laughing, "I've brought you a Smurfette!" Then he took you upstairs and plunged you into a scalding-hot bath. How long did you stay there? I don't remember; I just remember Adrien repeating to his mother, "Take it easy, Mum, take it easy! As soon as she's cooked, we can eat." It's true, we were hungry. I was hungry, anyway. And you know me, you know how old bastards are when they get hungry ... I was just about to say that we should start eating without you, when you came in, with wet hair and a shy smile, wearing one of Suzanne's old nightdresses.

'This time, your cheeks were red, red, red ...

'During dinner, you told us that you had met in the queue for the cinema, which was showing *A Sunday in the Country*, and that there were no more seats and that Adrien, the show-off – it runs in the family – offered you a real Sunday in the country, standing there in front of his motorcycle. It was a take-it-or-leave-it offer, and you took it, which explained your advanced state of frostbite because you had left Paris wearing only a T-shirt under your raincoat. Adrien was eating you up with his eyes, which was difficult for him since you kept looking down at the table. I could see a dimple when he spoke about you, and we imagined that you would smile at us ... I also remember those incredible sneakers you wore ...'

'Yellow Converses, oh God!'

'Right. That's why you have no right to criticise the

ones I bought for Lucie the other day ... That reminds me, I have to tell her ... "Don't listen to her, sweetie; when I met your mother, she was wearing yellow sneakers with red laces ..." '

'You even remember the laces?'

'I remember everything, Chloé, everything. The red laces, the book you read underneath the cherry tree while Adrien fixed his engine ...'

'Which was what?'

'*The World According to Garp*, right?'

'Exactly right.'

'I also remember how you volunteered to Suzanne to sweep the little stairway that led down to the old cellar. I remember the loving glances she threw you as she watched you wear yourself out over the thorns. You could read "Daughter-in-law? Daughter-in-law?" in big, flashing neon lights in front of her eyes. I drove you to the Saint-Amand market, you bought goat cheeses, and then we drank martinis in a café on the square. You read an article, about Andy Warhol I think, while Adrien and I played table soccer ...'

'It's unbelievable, how is it possible that you can remember all that?'

'Uhh ... I don't deserve much credit ... It's one of the few things that we share ...'

'You mean with Adrien?'

'Yes ...'

'Yes.'

*

I got up to get the cheese.

'No, no, don't change the plates, it's not worth it.'

'Of course it is! I know how you hate to eat your cheese from the same plate.'

'I hate that? Oh … It's true … Another thing old bastards do, right?'

'Ummm … Yes, that's right.'

He grimaced as he held out his plate.

'The hell with you.'

A dimple showed.

'Of course, I also remember your wedding day … You took my arm and you were so beautiful. You played with your hair. We were crossing that same square at Saint-Amand when you whispered in my ear: "You should kidnap me; I'd throw these horrible shoes out the window of your car and we'd go to Chez Yvette and eat seafood …" Your little joke made my head spin. I tightened my gloves. Here, serve yourself first …'

'No, no, you first.'

'What else can I tell you? I remember one day, we had arranged to meet in the café downstairs from my office so I could take back a ladle or some other such thing that Suzanne had lent you. I must have seemed disagreeable to you that day, I was in a hurry, preoccupied … I left before you had finished your tea. I asked you questions about your job and probably didn't pay attention to the answers.

That night at dinner, when Suzanne asked me, "What's new?" without really believing it, I answered, "Chloé is pregnant." "She told you?" "No, and I'm not sure that she knows it herself." Suzanne shrugged her shoulders and rolled her eyes, but I was right. A few weeks later, you told us the good news ...'

'How did you guess?'

'I don't know ... It seemed to me that your complexion had changed, that your fatigue was caused by something else ...'

I said nothing.

'I could go on and on like this. You see, you're not being fair – what were you just saying? That all this time, all these years, I never took an interest in you. Oh, Chloé, I hope you feel ashamed of yourself.'

Jokingly, he gave me a stern look.

'On the other hand, I am egotistical, you're right there. I told you I don't want you to go because I don't want you to go. I'm thinking of myself. You are closer to me than my own daughter. My daughter would never tell me that I'm an old bastard, she would just think to herself that I'm an idiot!'

He got up to get the salt.

'Hey now ... what's the matter?'

'Nothing. It's nothing.'

'Yes, it is. You're crying.'

'No, I'm not crying. Look, I'm not crying.'

'Yes, you are. You're crying! Do you want a glass of water?'

'Yes.'

'Oh, Chloé ... I don't want you to cry. It makes me unhappy.'

'There, you see! It's about you! You're just impossible ...'

I tried for a playful tone, but bubbles of mucus came out of my nose. It was pitiful.

I laughed. I cried. This wine wasn't cheering me up at all.

'I should never have talked to you about all that ...'

'No, it's okay. They're my memories, too ... I just have to get used to all this. It might be hard for you to understand, but this is totally new for me. Two weeks ago, I was still your common or garden wife and mother. I flipped through my diary on the Métro, planning dinner parties, and I filed my nails while thinking about holidays. I asked myself, "Should we take the girls, or go away just the two of us?" That kind of thing ...

'I also said to myself, "We should find another apartment; this one is nice, but it's too dark ..." I was waiting for Adrien to feel better, because I could see that he hadn't been himself recently ... Irritable, touchy, tired ... I was worried about him; I thought, "They're killing him at work, what's with the impossible hours?" '

He turned to face the fire.

*

'Common or garden, but not very sharp, right? I waited

65

to have dinner with him. I waited for hours. Sometimes I even fell asleep waiting for him … He would finally come home, wearing a long face, with his tail between his legs. I would yawn and stretch and guide him to the kitchen, bustling about. He wasn't hungry, of course, he had the decency to not have any appetite. Or maybe they had already eaten? Most likely …

'It must have been hell for him to sit across from me! What a trial I must have been with my cheerful nature and my soap opera stories about the goings-on of Firmin-Gédon Square. Torture for him, when I think of it … Lucie lost a tooth, my mother's not doing well, the Polish au pair girl who looks after little Arthur is going out with the neighbour's son, I finished my sculpture this morning, Marion cut her hair and it looks terrible, the teacher needs egg-boxes, you look tired, take a day off, give me your hand, do you want some more spinach? Poor thing … a form of torture for an unfaithful but scrupulous husband. What torture … But I didn't suspect a thing. I didn't see it coming, do you understand? How could I have been so blind? How? Either I was completely stupid or completely trusting. It amounts to the same thing, really …'

I leaned my chair back.

'Oh, Pierre … What a bad joke life is …'

'It's good, isn't it?'

'Very. Too bad it doesn't keep any of its promises …'

'It's the first time I've drunk it.'

'Me too.'

'It's like your rosebush; I bought it for the label ...'

'Mm. A bad joke ... What stupidity.'

'But you're still young ...'

'No, I'm old, I feel old. I'm all used up. I feel like I'm going to become wary. I'll watch my life through a peephole. I won't open the door. "Step back. Let me see your hands. That's good, now the other. Don't scuff the parquet. Stay in the hallway. Don't move." '

'No, you'll never become that kind of woman. As much as you might want to, you can't. People will keep walking into your life, you will continue to suffer and it's better that way. I'm not worried about you.'

'No, of course not.'

'What do you mean?'

'Of course you're not worried about me. You don't worry about people, ever ...'

'That's true, you're right. It's hard for me to care.'

'Why?'

'I don't know. Because other people don't interest me, I suppose ...'

'... except Adrien.'

'What do you mean, Adrien?'

'I think about him.'

'You worry about Adrien?'

'Yes, I think so ... Yes.

'At any rate, he's the one I worry about the most.'

'Why?'

'Because he's unhappy.'

I was completely taken aback.

'Well, now I've heard everything! He's not unhappy at all … On the contrary, he's very happy! He's traded in his boring, used wife for a brand-new, amusing model. His life is a lot more fun today, you know.'

I looked at my wrist.

'Let's see, what time is it? A quarter to ten. Where is our martyr now? Where could he be? At the movies, or the theatre perhaps? Or maybe they're having dinner somewhere. They must have finished their starter by now … He caresses her palm while dreaming about later. Careful, here comes the main course, she pulls her hand back and gives him a smile. Or perhaps they're in bed … That's most likely, isn't it? In the beginning one makes love a lot, if I remember correctly …'

'You're being cynical.'

'I'm protecting myself.'

'Whatever he's doing, he's unhappy.'

'Because of me, you mean? I'm spoiling his fun? Oh, that ungrateful woman …'

'No. Not because of you, because of him. Because of this life, which never does what you want it to. Our efforts are so laughable …'

'You're right, the poor thing …'

'You're not listening to me.'

'No.'

'Why aren't you listening to me?'

I bit into a piece of bread.

'Because you're a bulldozer, you flatten everything in your path ... For you, my sorrow is ... what? ... a burden, and soon it will start to get on your nerves. And then this thing about blood ties ... This stupid notion ... You didn't give a damn about taking your children in your arms, about telling them that you loved them even once, but despite this, I know that you'll always leap to their defence. No matter what they say or do, they will always be right in contrast to the rest of us barbarians – the ones who don't have the same name as you.

'Your children haven't given you a whole lot of reasons to be happy, but you're the only one who can criticise them. The only one! Adrien takes off and leaves me here with the girls. All right, that bothers you, but I've given up hope of hearing you speak a few harsh words against him. A few harsh words ... it wouldn't change anything, but it would give me a bit of pleasure. So much pleasure, if you only knew ... Yes, it's hopeless. I'm hopeless. But just a couple of heartfelt words, really bitter words, the ones you know so well how to say ... Why not for him? I deserve that, after all. I'm waiting for the condemnation of the patriarch seated at the head of the table. All these years I've listened to you divide up the world. The good and the bad, those who have earned your respect and those who haven't. All these years I've run up against your speeches, your authority, your commander-in-chief expressions, your silences ... So much arrogance. So much arrogance ... While all along being a pain in the arse, Pierre ...

'You see, I'm not that complicated a person and I need to hear you say, "My son is a bastard, and I ask for your forgiveness." I need that, do you understand?'

'Don't count on it.'

I cleared the plates.

'I wouldn't count on it.'

'Would you like dessert?'

'No.'

'You don't want anything?'

'So it's ruined ... I must have pulled on the wrong thread ...'

I wasn't listening any more.

'The knot is tightened, and here we are, further apart than ever. So I'm an old bastard ... A monster ... And what else?'

I was looking for the sponge.

'And what else?'

I looked him right in the eyes.

'Listen to me, Pierre; for years I lived with a man who couldn't stand up straight because his father hadn't given him the support he needed. When I met Adrien, he didn't dare do anything for fear of disappointing you. And everything he did disappointed me because he never did it for himself, he did it for you. To amaze you or to irritate you. To provoke you or to please you. It was pathetic. I was barely twenty years old and I gave up my life for him. To listen to him and stroke his neck when he finally opened up. I don't regret it, I couldn't do anything else, anyway. It made me sick to see someone abase himself like that. We spent whole nights unravelling things and putting them in perspective. I gave him a shaking-up. I told him a thousand times that he was taking the easy way out. The easy way out! We made resolutions and then we broke them, we made others, and then finally I quit my studies so that he could pick his up again. I rolled up my sleeves and for three years I dropped him off at the university before going off to waste time in the basement of the Louvre. It was our deal: I wouldn't complain as long as he didn't talk about you. I'm not special. I never said he was the best. I just loved him. Loved. Him. Do you know what I'm talking about?'

He said nothing.

'So, you can see why I'm a little unhappy today ...'

I wiped the sponge around his hands that were placed on the table.

'He got his confidence back; the prodigal son is a new man. He can sail his boat like a big boy, and here he is, discarding his old self, right under the nose of his big, bad father. You have to admit, it's a little rough?'

Silence.

'You have nothing to say?'

'No. I'm going to bed.'

71

I set the machine going.
'That's it, good night.'

...

I bit my cheeks.
I kept some dreadful things to myself.

I took my glass and went to sit on the couch. I took off my shoes and sank into the cushions. I got up to get the bottle from the table. I poked the fire, turned out the light, and buried myself there.

I regretted not being drunk yet.
I regretted being there.
I regretted ... I regretted so many things.
So many things ...

I laid my head on the armrest and closed my eyes.

'Are you asleep?'

'No.'

He went to pour himself a glass of wine and sat down in an armchair next to the sofa.

The wind continued to blow. We sat in the dark. We watched the fire.

From time to time, one of us took a drink and then the other followed suit.

We were neither happy nor sad. We were tired.

After a very long moment he said:

'You know, I wouldn't be the person you said I was if I had had more courage ...'

'I'm sorry?'

I already regretted having answered him. I didn't want to talk about this shit any more. I just wanted to be left in peace.

'Everyone always talks about the sorrow of those left behind, but did you ever consider the sorrow of the ones who leave?'

Here we go again, I thought to myself, what kind of crazy idea is he going to try and put over on me now, the old fool?

I looked around for my shoes.

'We'll talk about it tomorrow, Pierre, I'm going … I'm fed up with this.'

'The sorrow of those who cause unhappiness … We pity the ones who stay, we comfort them, but what about those who leave?'

'What else do they want?' I exploded. 'A medal? Words of encouragement?'

He wasn't listening to me.

'The courage of those who look in the mirror one morning and say to themselves: "Do I have the right to make a mistake?" Just those few words … The courage to look their lives in the face and see nothing settled or harmonious there. The courage to destroy everything, to smash it out of … out of selfishness? Out of pure selfishness? No, not that … So what is it? Survival instinct? A moment of lucidity? Fear of death?

'The courage to confront yourself just once in your life. Confront yourself. By yourself. Finally.

' "The right to make a mistake", it's just a little expression, one tiny little phrase, but who gives you that right?

'Who, if not yourself?'

His hands were trembling.

*

'I never gave it to myself … I never gave myself any right. Only duty. And look what I've become: an old bastard. An old bastard in the eyes of one of the precious few people for whom I have a bit of respect. What a fiasco …

'I've made lots of enemies. I'm not bragging, and I'm not complaining either. I just don't give a damn. But friends, those I wanted to please? There are so few, so few … and you're one of them. You, Chloé, because you have such a gift for life. You grab hold of it with both hands. You move, you dance, you know how to make the rain and the sunshine in a home. You have this incredible gift for making the people around you happy. You're so at ease, so at ease on this little planet …'

'I have the feeling we're not talking about the same person …'

He hadn't heard me.

He sat straight in his chair. He had stopped speaking. He hadn't crossed his legs, and his glass rested between his thighs.

I couldn't see his face.

His face was in the shadow of the armchair.

'I loved a woman … I'm not talking about Suzanne, I'm talking about another woman.'

I opened my eyes.

*

'I loved her more than anything. More than anything … I didn't know that someone could love that much. Or me, at any rate, I thought that I wasn't … *programmed* to love like that … Declarations, insomnia, the ravages of passion, all that was for other people. Besides, just the word "passion" made me snigger. Passion, passion! I filed that somewhere between "hypnosis" and "superstition" … The way I said it, it was practically a four-letter word. And then, it hit me at the moment when I least expected it. I … I loved a woman.

'I fell in love like you catch a cold. Without wanting to, without believing in it, against my will and with no way to defend myself, and then …'

He cleared his throat.

'And then I lost her. In the same way.'

…

I couldn't move. An anvil had just fallen on my head.

'Her name was Mathilde. Her name is still Mathilde, by the way. Mathilde Courbet. Like the painter …

'I was forty-two years old and I thought I was already old. I've always thought I was old. It's Paul who was young. Paul will always be young and handsome.

'I'm Pierre. Pierre the plodder, Pierre the hard worker.

76

'When I was ten years old, I already had the face I have today. The same haircut, the same glasses, the same gestures, the same little tics. At ten, I already changed my plate for the cheese course, I imagine ...'

In the dark, I smiled at him.

'Forty-two years old ... What can you expect from life at forty-two?

'Me, nothing. I expected nothing. I worked. More and more and always more. It was like camouflage for me, my armour and my alibi. My alibi for not living. Because I didn't like living all that much. I thought I didn't have a gift for it.

'I invented hardships for myself, mountains to climb. Very high ones, very steep. Then I rolled up my sleeves, climbed them, and then invented others. And yet, I wasn't ambitious, I just had no imagination.'

He took a sip of wine.

...

'I ... I didn't know anything about this, you know ... It was Mathilde who taught me. Oh, Chloé ... How I loved her ... How I loved her ... Are you still there?'

'Yes.'

'Are you listening to me?'

'Yes.'
'Am I boring you?'
'No.'
'Are you going to fall asleep?'
'No.'

He got up and put another log on the fire. He stayed crouched in front of the fireplace.

'You know what she complained about? That I was too talkative. Can you believe that? Me ... too talkative! Incredible, isn't it? But it was true ... I put my head on her stomach and I talked. I talked for hours, for whole days, even. I heard the sound of my voice grow deep beneath her skin and I loved it. I was a word machine ... I made her head spin. I inundated her with words. She laughed. She told me, "*Shhh, don't talk so much*, I can't listen to you any more. Why do you go on like that?"'

'I had forty-two years of silence to catch up on. Forty-two years of not speaking, of keeping everything to myself. What did you say a while ago? That my silence looks like disdain, wasn't that it? That hurt, but I can understand, I understand why people criticise me. I understand, but I have no interest in defending myself. That's the problem, really ... But disdain, I don't think so. As strange as it may seem, my silence is more like shyness. I don't like myself enough to attach the least importance to what I say. Think twice, speak once, as the old saying goes. I always think one too many times. People find me pretty discouraging ... I didn't like myself before Mathilde and I like myself even less since. I suppose I'm hard because of that ...'

He sat back down.

'I'm tough at work, but that's just because I'm playing a role, you see? I have to be tough, I have to make them think I'm a tyrant. Can you imagine if they discovered my secret? If they figured out that I'm shy? That I have to work three times harder than the others for the same result? That I have a bad memory? That I'm slow to understand? If they knew that, they'd eat me alive!

'Plus, I don't know how to make myself liked ... I have no charisma, as they say. If I give someone a rise, I do it in a curt voice; when someone thanks me, I don't answer. When I want to do something nice for someone, I stop myself, and if I have good news to announce, I let my secretary Françoise do it. When it comes to management, or human resources as they say, I'm a disaster, a complete disaster.

'It was Françoise who signed me up against my will for a sort of training course for hopeless bosses. What a lot of nonsense ... Shut up for two days at the Concorde Lafayette Hotel at Porte Maillot, being force-fed popular drivel by a shrink and an overexcited American. He sold his book at the end. *Work, Love, and Be the Best* it was called. My God, what a joke, now that I look back on it …

'At the end of the course, as I recall, they handed out diplomas for kind, understanding bosses. I gave it to Françoise, who pinned it up in the closet where we keep the cleaning products and toilet paper.

' "How was it?" she asked me.

' "It was pathetic."

'She smiled.

' "Listen, Françoise," I told her, "you're like God Almighty around here. Tell anyone who's interested that I'm not nice, but that they'll never lose their job because I'm very good at making the numbers work."

' "Amen," she murmured, bowing her head.

'And it was true. In twenty-five years of being a tyrant, I never had a strike and I never laid anyone off. Even when things were so bad in the early nineties, I never laid off a soul. Not one, do you understand?'

'And Suzanne?'

He was silent.

'Why are you so hard with her?'

'You think I'm hard?'

'Yes.'

'Hard in what way?'

'Hard.'

He rested his head on the armchair again.

'When Suzanne figured out that I had been unfaithful to her, it had already been over for a long time. I had … I'll tell you that later … In those years, we lived on Rue de la Convention. I didn't like the apartment. I didn't like the way she had decorated it. It was suffocating: too much furniture, too many knick-knacks, too many photos of us, too much of everything. I'm telling you this, but it's not important. I went back to that apartment to sleep and because my family lived there, period. One evening, she asked me to take her out to dinner. We went to a place just down the street, a horrible pizzeria. The neon lights made her look awful, and since she was already wearing the face of an outraged wife, they didn't help. It was cruel, but I hadn't done it on purpose, you see. I opened the door of the first cheap place I saw … I knew what was coming, and I had no desire to be far from my bed. And, as it turns out, it didn't take her long to get started. She had barely laid down the menu when she broke down sobbing.

'She knew everything. That it was a younger woman. She knew how long it had lasted and understood why I was always away from home now. She couldn't take it any longer. I was a monster. Did she deserve this much contempt? Did she deserve to be treated this way? Like a scullery maid? At first, she had looked the other way. She suspected something, but she trusted me. She thought it was just one of those things, a thrill, the need to seduce. Something to bolster my virility. And then there was my job. My work, so exhausting, so hard. And she – she had been occupied with setting up the new house. She couldn't manage everything at once. She couldn't fight every fire!

She had trusted me! And then I had fallen ill and she had looked the other way. But now, now she couldn't take it any more. No, she couldn't take me any more. My egotism, my contempt, the way in which – At that exact moment, the waiter interrupted her and, within a split second, she had switched masks. With a smile, she asked him a question about the tortellini something-or-other. I was fascinated. When he turned to me, I managed to stammer out, "The ... the same as Madame." I hadn't given the damn menu a single thought, you see. Not for a second ...'

'That was when I took the full measure of Suzanne's strength. Her immense strength. She's like a steamroller. That was when I knew that she was by far the sturdier of the two of us, and that nothing could really touch her. In fact, all of this was about her personal timetable. She was taking me to task because her beach house was finally finished. The last picture had been hung, the last curtain rod put up, and she finally turned in my direction and had been horrified by what she had discovered.

'I barely said a word, I defended myself half-heartedly. As I told you, I had already lost Mathilde by that point ...'

'I looked across the table at my wife getting upset in a miserable pizzeria in the fifteenth arrondissement in Paris, and I turned off the sound.'

'She gesticulated, let big tears roll down her cheeks, blew

her nose, and wiped her plate with a piece of bread. All the while, I twirled two or three strands of spaghetti around my fork without ever managing to raise them to my mouth. I also wanted very much to cry, but I stopped myself ...'

'Why did you stop yourself?'

'A question of upbringing, I suppose ... And I still felt so fragile ... I couldn't take the risk of letting myself go. Not there. Not then. Not with her. Not in that awful place. I was ... How can I put it ... barely in one piece.

'Then she told me that she had gone to see a lawyer to start divorce proceedings. Suddenly I started paying attention. A lawyer? Suzanne was asking for a divorce? I never imagined that things had gone that far, that she had been hurt that much ... She went to see a woman, the sister-in-law of one of her friends. She had hesitated but on the way back from a weekend here, she had made up her mind. She had decided in the car, when I hadn't spoken to her once except to ask if she had change for the motorway toll. She had invented a sort of conjugal Russian roulette: if Pierre speaks to me, I'll stay; if he doesn't, I'll divorce him.

'I was disconcerted. I never thought she was the gambling type.

'She pulled herself together and looked at me more self-confidently. Of course, she wanted to lay it all out. My trips, ever longer and more frequent, my lack of interest in family life, my neglected children, the report cards I never signed. All the lost years she had spent organising everything around me. For my well-being, for the company. The company that belonged to her family, to her, incidentally, the sacrifices she had made. How she had cared for my poor mother right up until the end. Everything really, everything she needed to say, plus everything that lawyers like to hear in order to put a price tag on the whole mess.

'But with that, I felt my old self again. We were now on familiar territory. What did she want? Money? How much? If she had given me a figure, I would have had my chequebook on the table.

'But no, she had my number, did I think I could get out of it that easily? I was so pathetic ... She started to cry again between mouthfuls of tiramisu. Why couldn't I understand anything? Life wasn't just about power struggles. Money couldn't buy everything. Or buy everything back. Was I going to pretend that I didn't understand anything? Didn't I have a heart? I was really pathetic. Pathetic ...

' "But why don't you ask for a divorce?" I finally blurted out, exasperated. "I'll take all the blame. All of it, you hear? Even how awful my mother was, I'll be glad to sign something and acknowledge it if that would make you happy, but please don't drag the lawyers into it, I beg you. Tell me how much you want instead."

'I had cut her to the quick.

'She lifted her head and looked me in the eye. It was the

first time in years that we had looked at each other that long. I searched for something else in her face. Our youth, perhaps ... A time when I didn't make her cry. When I didn't make any woman cry, and when the very idea of sitting at a table and hashing out one's love life seemed inconceivable.

'But there was nothing there, only the slightly sad expression of a defeated spouse who was about to make a confession. She hadn't gone back to see the lawyer because she didn't have the heart. She loved her life, her house, her children, her neighbourhood shops ... She was ashamed to admit it, and yet it was true: she didn't have the courage to leave me.

'The courage.

'I could run after women if that pleased me, I could have affairs if that was reassuring, but she – she wasn't leaving. She didn't want to lose what she had. Her social standing. Our friends, our relations, our children's friends. And then there was her brand-new house, where we hadn't even spent one night ... It was a risk she didn't want to take. After all, what good would it do? There were men who had cheated on their wives ... Lots of them, even ... She had finally told her story and had been disappointed by how banal it was. That's just how things were. The fault lay in what hangs between our legs. She just had to grin and bear it, let the storm pass. She had taken the first step, but the idea of no longer being Mrs Pierre Dippel had drained her of her courage. That was how it was, and too bad for her. Without the children, without me, she wasn't worth much.

'I offered her my handkerchief. "It's all right," she added, forcing herself to smile. "It's all right ... I'm staying with you because I couldn't think of a better idea. For once, I was badly organised. Me, the one who always anticipates everything. I ... It was too much for me, I suppose." She smiled through her tears.

'I patted her hand. It was finished. I was here. I wasn't with anyone else. No one. It was over. It was over ...'

'Over coffee we chatted about the owner's moustache and how awful the décor was.

'Two old friends covered with scars.

'We had lifted up a huge rock and had let it fall back immediately.

'It was too awful to look at what was crawling underneath.'

•••

'That night, in the darkness, I took Suzanne chastely in my arms. I couldn't do any more than that.

'For me, it was another sleepless night. Her confession, instead of reassuring me, had left me completely shaken. I have to say, I was in a terrible way at the time. Terrible, really terrible. Everything set me on edge. I found myself in a completely depressing situation: I had lost the woman I loved and had just learned that I had hurt the other one.

What a scene … I had lost the love of my life to stay with a woman who would never leave me because of her cheese shop and her butcher. It was impossible, everything was destroyed. Neither Mathilde nor Suzanne had deserved that. I had ruined everything. I had never felt so miserable in all my life …

'The medications I was taking didn't make things any easier, that's for certain, but if I had had more courage, I would have hanged myself that night.'

He tipped his head back to drain his glass.

'But Suzanne? She's not unhappy with you …'

'Oh, you think so? How can you say something like that? Did she say that she was happy?'

'No. Not like that. She didn't say it, but she gave me to understand … Anyway, she's not the type of woman to stop for a moment to ask herself if she is happy …'

'You're right, she isn't the type … That's where her strength lies, by the way. You know, if I was so miserable that night, it was really on account of her. When I see what she has turned into … So bourgeois, so conventional … If you could have seen what a little number she was when I met her … I'm not happy with what I did, really, it's nothing to be proud of. I suffocated her. I wilted her. For me, she was always the one who was there. Within reach. Close to hand. On the end of the phone. With the children. In the kitchen. A sort of vestal who spent the money that I earned and made our little world go around comfortably and without complaining. I never looked any further than the end of my nose.

'Which of her secrets had I found out? None. Did I ask her about herself, about her childhood, her memories, her regrets, her weariness, our physical relations, her faded hopes, her dreams? No. Never. Nothing. I wasn't interested.'

'Don't take it too much to heart, Pierre. You can't carry all the blame. Self-flagellation has its charms, but still ... You don't make a very convincing Saint Sebastian, you know ...'

'I like that, you don't let me get away with anything. You're the one who keeps me straight ... That's why I hate to lose you. Who's going to take a shot at me when you're no longer here?'

'We'll have lunch together every once in a while ...'

'Promise?'

'Yes.'

'You say that but you'll never do it, I know ...'

'We'll make a ritual out of it, the first Friday of the month, for example ...'

'Why Friday?'

'Because I love a good fish dish! You'll take me to good restaurants, right?'

'The best!'

'All right, now I'm reassured ... But it won't be for a long time ...'

'A long time?'
'Yes.'
'How long?'
I said nothing.
'Fine. I can wait.'

I poked at a log.

'To come back to Suzanne … Her bourgeois side, as you say. You had nothing to do with it, and it's a good thing. There are some things that are all hers without any of your help. It's like those English products that proclaim "By appointment to Her Majesty the Queen". Suzanne became who she is without any need for your "appointment". You can be annoying, but you're not all-powerful! That Lady Bountiful routine of hers, chasing after sales and recipes, she didn't need you to create that whole show for her. It comes naturally, as they say. It's in her blood, that *I dust, I remark, I judge, and I forgive* side of her. It's exhausting; it exhausts me, anyway – the parcelling out of her good deeds, and God knows she has plenty of good deeds, right?'

'Yes. God knows … Would you like something to drink?'

'No, thanks.'

'Some herbal tea, perhaps?'

'No, no. I'm fine getting slowly drunk …'

'All right then, I'll leave you in peace.'

'Pierre?'

'Yes?'

'I can't get over it.'

'Over what?'

'What you've just told me …'

'I can't either.'

'And Adrien?'

'What about him?'

'Will you tell him?'

'What would I tell him?'

'Well … all of that …'

'Adrien came to see me, believe it or not.'

'When?'

'Last week, and … I didn't tell him about it. I mean, I didn't talk about myself, but I listened …'

'What did he tell you?'

'What I told you, what I already knew … That he was unhappy, that he didn't know where he was going anymore …'

'He came to confide in you?!'

'Yes.'

I began to cry again.

'Does that surprise you?'

I shook my head.

'I feel betrayed. Even you … You … I hate that. I would never do that to someone, I –'

'Calm down. You're mixing everything up. Who said anything about betrayal? Where is the treason? He showed up without warning, and as soon as I saw him I suggested that we go out. I switched off my mobile and we went down to the parking garage. As soon as I started up the car, he said to me, "I'm going to leave Chloé." I remained calm. We drove up into the open air. I didn't want to ask questions, I waited for him to speak ... Always this problem of which thread to pull ... I didn't want to rush things. I didn't know what to do. I was a bit shaken up, to tell you the truth. I turned on to the Paris ring road and opened the ashtray.'

'And then?' I added.

'And then nothing. He's married, he has two children. He had thought it over. He thought that it was worth –'

'Shut up, please shut up ... I know the rest.'

I got up to get the roll of paper towels.

'You must be proud of him, eh? It's great what he did, right? There's a man for you! What courage. What sweet revenge – he really got you there! What sweet revenge ...'

'Don't use that tone of voice.'

'I'll use any tone I want, and I'm going to tell you what I think ... You're even worse than he is. You, you ruined everything. Oh yes, beneath your high-minded attitude, you've ruined everything and you're using him, using his sleeping around to comfort yourself. I think that's pathetic. You make me sick, both of you.'

'You're talking nonsense. You know that, don't you? You know that you're talking nonsense?'

He spoke to me very gently.

'If it was just a question of sleeping around, as you say, we wouldn't be here, and you know it …

'Chloé, talk to me.'

'I'm a royal bitch … No, don't contradict me for once. It would make me very happy for you to not contradict me.'

'Can I make a confession? A very difficult confession?'

'Go ahead, given the state I'm in …'

'I think that it's a good thing.'

'That what's a good thing?'

'What's happened to you …'

'Becoming a royal bitch?'

'No, that Adrien left. I think that you deserve better … Better than this forced happiness … Better than filing your nails in the Métro while flipping through your diary, better than Firmin-Gédon Square, better than what the two of you had become. It's shocking that I'm telling you this, isn't it? And what business is it of mine, anyway? It's shocking, but too bad. I'm not going to pretend, I care about you too much. I don't think that Adrien was in your class. He was a little out of his league with you. That's what I think …

'I know, it's shocking because he's my son and I shouldn't talk about him that way. But there you are, I'm an old bastard and I don't give a damn about appearances. I'm telling you this because I believe in you. You … You weren't really properly loved. And if you could be as honest as I am right this minute, you'd act offended, but you'd think exactly the same thing.'

'You're talking nonsense.'

'And there you are. That little offended air of yours …'

'So now you're a psychoanalyst?'

'Haven't you ever heard that little voice inside that pokes you from time to time, to remind you that you weren't really properly loved?'

'No.'

'No?'

'No.'

'All right. I guess I'm wrong …'

He leaned forward, pressing on his knees.

'I think that someday you should come up out of there.'

'Out of where?'

'That basement.'

'You really do have an opinion about everything, don't you?'

'No. Not about everything. Why are you slaving away in the basement of a museum when you know what you're capable of? It's a waste of time. What is it you do? Copies? Plaster casts? You're tinkering. Who cares? And how long are you going to do it? Until you retire? Don't tell me you're happy in that hellhole stuffed with civil servants …'

'No, no, ' I said ironically, 'I would never say that, rest assured.'

'If I were your lover, I would grab you by the scruff of the neck and drag you back up into the light. You're really talented with your hands and you know it. Accept it. Accept your gifts. Take responsibility. I would sit you down somewhere and tell you, "It's up to you now. It's your move, Chloé. Show us what you're made of." '

'And what if there's nothing?'

'Well, it would be the moment to find out. And stop biting your lip, it hurts me.'

'Why is it you have so many good ideas for other people and so few for yourself?'

'I've already answered that question.'

'What is it?'

    'I thought I heard Marion crying.'

    'I didn't h—'

    'Shhh.'

'It's okay, she's gone back to sleep.'

    I sat back down and pulled the blanket over me.

    'Shall I go and see?'

    'No, no. Let's wait a little.'

'And what do you think I deserve, Mr Know-It-All?'

    'You deserve to be treated like what you are.'

    'Which is … ?'

    'Like a princess. A modern princess.'

    'Pfff … That's ridiculous.'

'Yes, I'm prepared to say anything. Anything if that makes you smile … Smile for me, Chloé.'

'You're crazy.'

He got up.

'Ah … that's perfect! I like that better. You starting to say fewer stupid things … Yes, I am crazy, and you know what I say? I'm crazy and I'm hungry. What could I eat for dessert?'

'Look in the fridge. You'll have to finish the girls' yogurts …'

'Where are they?'

'Down on the bottom.'

'Those little pink things?'

'Yes.'

'It's not so bad …'

He licked his spoon.

'Do you see what they're called?'

'No.'

'Look, specially for you.'

'*Little Rascals* … That's cute.'

...

'We should probably go to bed, don't you think?'

'Yes.'

'Are you sleepy?'

I was upset.

'How can you expect me to sleep with everything that's been churned up? I feel like I'm stirring a huge cauldron …'

'I untie knots while you stir your cauldron. It's funny, the images we use …'

'You the mathematician and me the crone.'

'The crone? Rubbish. My princess a crone … The number of ridiculous things you've said tonight.'

'You're a pain in the neck, aren't you?'

'Very much so.'

'Why?'

'I don't know. Perhaps because I say what I think. It's not all that common … I'm no longer afraid of not being liked.'

'What about by me?'

'Oh, you; you like me, I'm not worried about that!'

'Pierre?'

'Yes?'

'What happened with Mathilde?'

He looked at me. He opened his mouth and closed it again. He crossed and uncrossed his legs. He got up. He poked the fire and stirred the embers. He lowered his head and murmured:

'Nothing. Nothing happened. Or very little. So few days, so few hours … Almost nothing, really.'

'You don't want to talk about it?'

'I don't know.'

'You never saw her again?'

'Yes, once. A few years ago. In the gardens of the Palais-Royal ...'

'And then?'

'And then nothing.'

'How did you meet her?'

'You know ... if I start, I don't know when I'll stop.'

'I told you I wasn't sleepy.'

He began to examine Paul's drawing. The words didn't come easily.

...

'When was it?'

'It was ... I saw her for the first time on June 8, 1978, in Hong Kong at about eleven o'clock, local time. We met on the nineteenth floor of the Hyatt Tower in the office of a Mr Singh, who needed me to drill somewhere in Taiwan. You find this funny?'

'Yes, because it's so precise. She worked with you?'

'She was my translator.'

'From Chinese?'

'No, from English.'

'But you speak English, don't you?'

'Not well. Not well enough to handle this type of thing; it was too subtle. When you get to that level, it's no longer language, it's like magic tricks. You miss one innuendo and you're out of your depth. What's more, I didn't know the exact terms to translate the technical jargon we were using that day, and to top it off, I could never get used to the Chinese accent. I feel like I hear "ting ting" at the end of every word. Not to mention the words that I don't even understand.'

'And so?'

'And so I was confused. I had expected to be working with an old Englishman, a local translator with whom Françoise had flirted on the phone, "You'll see, he's a real gentleman …"'

'My foot! There I was, under pressure, jet-lagged, anxious, tied up in knots, shaking like a leaf, and not an Englishman in sight. It was a huge deal, enough to keep the business going for two years. I don't know if you can understand …'

'What were you selling, exactly?'

'Storage tanks.'

'Storage tanks?'

'Yes, but wait. These weren't just ordinary storage tanks, they were –'

'No, no, I don't care! Keep going!'

'So, as I said, I was at the end of my rope. I had worked on this project for months, and I had a huge amount of money tied up in it. I had put the company in debt, and I had even invested my personal savings. With this deal, I could slow the closing of a factory near Nancy. Eighteen employees. I had Suzanne's brothers on my back; I knew they wanted to get even, and they were not going to cut me any slack, those useless – What's more, I had a

ferocious case of diarrhoea. I'm sorry to be so prosaic, but
… Anyway, I walked into that office as if I were going
into battle, and when I learned that I was putting my life
in the hands of … of … this creature, I nearly passed out.'

'But why?'

'The oil business is a very macho world, you see. It has
changed somewhat now, but at the time, you didn't see
many women.'

'And you too …'

'What about me?'

'You're a little macho yourself.'

He didn't say no.

'Hold on – Put yourself in my place for a moment. I was
expecting to be greeted by an old phlegmatic Englishman,
someone with a moustache and a rumpled suit who was
well versed in the colonial ways of doing things, and there
I was shaking the hand of a young woman and casting
sidelong glances at her décolleté … No, believe me, it
was too much. I didn't need that … I felt the ground give
way under my feet. She explained that Mr Magoo was ill,
that they had sent for her yesterday evening, and then she
shook my hand very hard to give me strength. Anyway,
that's what she told me afterwards: that she had shaken me
until my teeth rattled because she thought I looked rather
pale.'

'His name was really Mr Magoo?'

'No. I'm just making that up.'

'What happened next?'

'I whispered in her ear: "But I hope you're aware ... I mean, of the technical data ... It's pretty specific ... I don't know if they alerted you ..." And then she gave me this marvellous smile. The type of smile that more or less says, "Shhh ... Don't try to confuse me, my dear man."

'I was devastated.

'I leaned into her lovely little neck. She smelled good. She smelled wonderfully good ... Everything was mixed up in my head. It was a catastrophe. She sat across from me, just to the right of a vigorous Chinese man who had me by the balls, if you'll pardon the expression. She rested her chin on her crossed fingers and threw me confident glances to give me strength. There was something cruel in those little half-smiles; I was completely in a daze and I was aware of it. I stopped breathing. I crossed my arms over my stomach to cover my paunch and prayed to heaven. I was at her mercy, and I was about to live the most wonderful hours of my life.'

'You tell a good story ...'

'You're making fun of me.'

'No, no! Not at all!'

'Yes, you are. You're making fun of me. I'll stop.'

'No, please! Absolutely not. And then what happened?'

'You broke my momentum.'

'I won't say anything more.'

He was silent.

'And then?'

'And then what?'

'And then how did it go with Mr Singh?'

*

'You're smiling. Why are you smiling? Tell me!'

'I'm smiling because it was incredible ... Because she was incredible ... Because the whole situation was completely incredible ...'

'Stop smiling to yourself ! Tell me, Pierre! Tell me!'

'Well ... First she pulled a case from her bag, a small, plastic, imitation-crocodile glasses case. She did it very self-importantly. Then she balanced a horrible pair of spectacles on her nose. You know, those severe little glasses with white metal frames. The kind that retired schoolteachers wear. And from that moment on, her face closed up. She ceased to look at me in the same way. She held my gaze and waited for me to recite my lesson.

'I talked, she translated. I was fascinated because she started her sentences before I finished mine. I don't know how she pulled it off; it was a tour de force. She listened and spoke nearly at the same time. It was simultaneous translation. It was fascinating ... Really ... At first, I spoke slowly, and then more and more quickly. I think that I was trying to rattle her a bit. She didn't bat an eye. On the contrary, she got a kick out of finishing my sentences before I did. She was already making me feel just how predictable I was ...

'And then she got up to translate some charts on a board. I took advantage of the situation to look at her legs. She had a little old-world side to her, outmoded, completely anachronistic. She was wearing a plaid knee-length skirt, a dark green twinset, and – Now why are you laughing?'

'Because you used the word "twinset". It makes me laugh.'

'Really, I don't see what's so funny! What else am I supposed to say?'

'Nothing, nothing …'

'You're such a pain …'

'I'll be quiet, I'll be quiet.'

'Even her brassiere was old-fashioned. She had pushed-up breasts like the girls in my youth. They were nice, not too large, slightly spread, pointed … Pushed up. And I was fascinated by her stomach. A round little stomach, round like a bird's belly. An adorable little stomach that stretched the squares on her skirt and that I found … I could already feel it beneath my hands … I was trying to get a glimpse of her feet when I saw she was upset. She had stopped speaking. She was completely pink. Her forehead, her cheeks, her neck were pink. Pink as a little shrimp. She looked at me, alarmed.

' "What's happening?" I asked her.

' "You … Didn't you understand what he said?"

' "Um … no. What did he say?"

' "You didn't understand or you didn't hear?"

' "I … I don't know … I didn't hear, I think …" '

'She stared at the ground. She was overcome. I imagined

the worst, a disaster, a mistake, a huge blunder … While she straightened her hair, in my mind I was already closing down the business.

' "What's happened? Is there a problem?"

' Mr. Singh laughed, said something to her that I still couldn't understand. I was completely lost. I didn't understand a thing. I looked like a complete idiot!

' "But what did he say? Tell me what he said!"

' She stammered.'

' "It's hopeless, is that it?"

' "No, no, I don't think so …"

' "Then what is it?"

' "Mr Singh is wondering if it is a good idea to discuss such an important deal with you today …"

' "But why? What is not going right?"

'I turned to him to reassure him. I nodded idiotically, and tried the winning smile of a confident French businessman. I must have seemed ridiculous … And the big boss just kept on laughing … He was so pleased with himself that you couldn't see his eyes.

' "Did I say something wrong?"

' "No."

' "Did you say something wrong?"

' "Me? Of course not! All I'm doing is repeating your gobbledygook."

' "Then what is it?"

'I could feel sweat running down my sides.

'She laughed and fanned herself. She seemed a bit nervous.

' "Mr Singh says that you are not concentrating."

' "But I am, I am concentrating! I am concentrating very hard!" I even said it in English. "*I am very concentrated!* "

' "*No, no,*" he answered in English, shaking his head.

' "Mr Singh says that you are not concentrating because you are falling in love, and Mr Singh does not want to do business with a Frenchman who is falling in love. He says that it is too dangerous."

'It was my turn to go crimson.

' "No, no …" I said it again, in English. "*I'm fine, I mean, I am calm … I … I …*" I was speaking a mixture of English and French.

'And to her I said:

'"Tell him that it is not true. That it's fine. That everything is fine. Tell him that … *I am okay. Yes, yes, I'm okay.*"

'I fidgeted.

'She smiled one of those little smiles from earlier.

' "That it's not true?"

'What kind of shit had I got myself into?

' "No, I mean, yes, uh … no, I mean that's not the problem … I mean, that's not a problem … I … *There IS no problem, I am fine!* "

'I think they were all making fun of me. The big boss, his associates, and this young lady.

'She didn't try to make it easy on me:

' "Is it true or not true?"

'The bitch! Was this really the moment?

' "It's not true," I lied.

' "Oh, all right then! You had me worried …"

'The bitch, I thought again to myself.

'She had me completely floored.'

'And then?'

'And then we got back to work. Very professionally. As though nothing had happened. I was drenched with sweat. I felt as if someone had electrocuted me and I had definitely lost my edge … I didn't look at her any more. I didn't want to. I wished that she didn't exist. I couldn't turn in her direction. I wanted her to disappear down a hole and to disappear with her. And the more I ignored her, the more I fell in love with her. It was exactly like I told you a while ago, like a sickness. You know how it goes: you sneeze once, twice. You shiver, and boom. It's too late. What's done is done. It was the same thing: I was caught, I was done for. It was hopeless and when she repeated the words of old Mr Singh, I plunged into my files headfirst. She must have had fun. This ordeal lasted nearly three hours … What is it? Are you cold?'

'A little, but I'm fine, I'm okay … Go on. What happened then?'

He leaned over to help me pull up the cover.

'After that, nothing. Afterwards … I told you, I had already experienced the best part … Afterwards I … It was … Afterwards it got sadder.'

'But not right away?'

'No, not right away. There were still some good times … But all the moments we shared after that meeting, it was as if I had stolen them …'

'Stolen them from whom?'

'From whom? From what? If only I knew …

'Afterwards, I gathered up my papers and put the cap back on my pen. I got up, I shook the hands of my tormentors and left the room. And in the lift, when the doors closed, I really felt as if I had fallen down a hole. I was exhausted, empty, totally wrung out and on the verge of tears. Nerves, I suppose … I felt so miserable, so alone … Alone, above all. I went back to my hotel room, ordered a whisky and ran a bath. I didn't even know her name. I knew nothing about her. I made a list of what I did know: she spoke remarkably good English. She was intelligent … Very intelligent … Perhaps too intelligent? I was flabbergasted by her technical, scientific, and steel-making knowledge. She was a brunette. She was very pretty. She was … let's see … about five foot four. She made fun of me. She wasn't wearing a wedding ring and she gave the impression of having the cutest little stomach. She … what else? I began to lose hope as my bath cooled.

'That evening, I went to dinner with some of the men from Comex. I ate nothing. I agreed with everything, and answered yes or no without knowing what I was saying. She haunted me.

'She haunted me, do you understand?'

He knelt in front of the fire and slowly worked the bellows.

'When I returned to the hotel, the receptionist handed me a message with my key. In small handwriting I read:

It wasn't true?

'She was sitting at the bar, watching me and smiling.

'I walked over, lightly hitting myself in the chest.

'My poor heart had stopped and I was trying to get it working again.

'I was so happy. I hadn't lost her. Not yet.

'So happy and also surprised because she had changed her outfit. Now she was wearing an old pair of blue jeans and a shapeless T-shirt.

' "You changed your clothes?"

' "Um ... yes."

' "But why?"

' "When you saw me earlier, I was in a sort of disguise. I dress that way when I work with old-school Chinese types. I figured out that the old-fashioned look pleased them, reassured them ... I don't know ... They feel more confident ... I dress up like a maiden aunt and I become harmless."

' "But you didn't look like a maiden aunt, I can assure you! You ... You were just fine ... You ... I ... I mean, it's a shame –"

' "That I changed clothes?"

' "Yes."

' "So you like me harmless, too?"

'She smiled. I melted.

' "I don't think that you are any less dangerous in your little plaid skirt. I don't think so at all, not in the least little bit." '

'We ordered Chinese beers. Her name was Mathilde, she was thirty years old, and although she had astounded me, she couldn't take all the credit: her father and her two brothers worked for Shell. She knew the jargon by heart. She had lived in every oil-producing country in the world, had gone to fifty schools, and knew how to swear in every language. She couldn't say exactly where she lived. She owned nothing, just memories. And friends. She loved her work, translating thoughts and juggling with words. She was in Hong Kong at the moment because all she had to do to find work was hold out her hand. She loved that city where the skyscrapers spring up overnight and where you can eat in some cheap joint just a few steps down the road. She loved the energy of the place. She had spent a few years in France when she was a child, and occasionally returned to see her cousins. One day she would buy a house there. It didn't really matter what kind of house or where, as long as there were cows and a fireplace. She laughed as she said that, because she was afraid of cows! She stole cigarettes from me and answered all my questions by first rolling her eyes. She asked me a few, but I ducked them. I wanted to listen to her, I wanted to hear the sound of her voice, that slight accent, her way of putting things that was hesitant and old-fashioned. I took it all in. I wanted to immerse myself in her, in her face. I already adored her neck, her hands, the shape of her nails, her slightly rounded forehead, her adorable little nose, her beauty marks, the dark circles under her eyes, those serious eyes … I was completely head over heels. You're smiling again.'

'I don't recognise you.'

'Are you still cold?'

'No, it's fine.'

'She fascinated me … I wanted the world to stop turning, for the night to never end. I didn't want to leave her. Not ever. I wanted to stay slumped in that armchair and listen to her recount her life until the end of time. I wanted the impossible. Without knowing it, I had set the tone of our relationship … time in suspension, unreal, impossible to hold on to, to retain. Impossible to savour, too. And then she got up. She had to be at work early in the morning. For Singh and Co. again. She really loved that old fox, but she had to get some sleep, because he was tough! I stood up at the same time. My heart failed me again. I was afraid of losing her. I mumbled something while she put on her jacket.

' "Excuse me?"

' "Imafrloosngou."

' "What did you say?"

' "I said I'm afraid of losing you." '

'She smiled. She said nothing. She smiled and swung lightly back and forth, holding on to the collar of her jacket. I kissed her. Her mouth was closed. I kissed her smile. She shook her head and gently gave me a little push.

'I could have fallen over backwards.'

...

'That's all?'

'Yes.'

'You don't want to tell me the rest, is that it? It gets X-rated?'

'Not at all! Not at all, my dear ... She left and I sat back down. I spent the rest of the night in a reverie, smoothing her little note on my thigh. Nothing very steamy, you see ...'

'Oh! Well, anyway ... it was your thigh ...'

'My dear, how stupid you are.'

I giggled.

'But why did she come back, then?'

'That's exactly what I asked myself that night, and the next day, and the day after and all the other days until I saw her again ...'

'When did you see her next?'

'Two months later. She landed in my office one evening in the middle of August. I wasn't expecting anyone. I had come back from holiday a little early to work while things were calm. The door opened and it was her. She had dropped by just like that. By chance. She had just been in Normandy, and was waiting for a friend to call to know when she would leave again. She looked me up in the telephone directory and there she was.

'She brought back a pen I had left halfway around the world. She had forgotten to give it to me in the bar, but this time she remembered it at once and was digging around in her bag.

'She hadn't changed. I mean, I hadn't idealised her, and I asked her:

' "But ... you came just for that? Because of the pen?"

' "Yes, of course. It's a beautiful pen. I thought you might be attached to it."

'She held it out to me, smiling. It was a Bic. A red Bic biro.

'I didn't know what to do. I ... She took me in her arms and I was overcome. The world was all mine.'

'We walked across Paris holding hands. Along the Seine, from the Trocadero all the way to the Ile de la Cité. It was a magnificent evening. It was hot, and the light was soft. The sun never seemed to set. We were like two tourists, carefree, filled with wonder, coats slung over our shoulders and fingers entwined. I played tour guide. I hadn't walked like that in years. I rediscovered my city. We ate at the Place Dauphine and spent the following days in her hotel room. I remember the first evening. Her salty taste. She must have bathed right before taking the train. I got up in the night because I was thirsty. I … It was marvellous.

'It was marvellous and completely false. Nothing was real. This wasn't life. This wasn't Paris. It was the month of August. I wasn't a tourist. I wasn't single. I was lying. I was lying to myself, to her, to my family. She wasn't fooled, and when the party was over, when it was time for the telephone calls and the lies, she left.

'At the boarding gate, she told me:

' "I'm going to try to live without you. I hope I'll find a way …"

'I didn't have the courage to kiss her.'

'That evening, I ate at the Drugstore. I was suffering. I was suffering as if part of me was missing, as though someone had cut off an arm or a leg. It was an incredible sensation. I didn't know what had happened to me. I remember that I drew two silhouettes on a paper napkin. The one on the left was her from the front, and the one on the right was her from the back. I tried to remember the exact location of her beauty marks, and when the waiter came over and saw all those little dots, he asked if I was an acupuncturist. I didn't know what had happened to me, but I knew it was something serious! For several days, I had been myself. Nothing more or less than myself. When I was with her, I had the impression that I was a good guy … It was as simple as that. I didn't know that I could be a good guy.

'I loved this woman. I loved this Mathilde. I loved the

sound of her voice, her spirit, her laugh, her take on the world, that sort of fatalism you see in people who have been everywhere. I loved her laugh, her curiosity, her discretion, her spinal column, her slightly bulging hips, her silences, her tenderness, and ... all the rest. Everything ... Everything. I prayed that she wouldn't be able to live without me. I wasn't thinking about the consequences of our encounter. I had just discovered that life was much more joyful when you were happy. It took me forty-two years to find it out, and I was so dazzled that I forced myself not to ruin everything by fixing my gaze on the horizon. I was on cloud nine.'

He refilled our glasses.

'From that moment on, I became a workaholic. I spent most of my time in the office. I was the first to arrive and the last to leave. I worked on Saturdays, and couldn't wait for Sundays to be over. I invented all kinds of pretexts. I finally landed the contract with Taiwan and was able to manoeuvre more freely. I took advantage of the situation to pile on extra projects, more or less sensible. And all of it, all of those insane days and hours were for one reason: because I hoped that she would call.

'Somewhere on the planet there was a woman – perhaps around the corner, perhaps ten thousand kilometres away – and the only thing that mattered was that she would be able to reach me.

'I was confident and full of energy. I think I was fairly happy at that time in my life because even if I wasn't with her, I knew she existed. That was already incredible.

'A few days before Christmas, I heard from her. She was coming to France and asked if I would be free for lunch the following week. We decided to meet in the same little wine bar. However, it was no longer summer, and when she reached for my hand, I swiftly drew it back. "Do they know you here?" she asked, hiding a smile.

'I had hurt her. I was so unhappy. I gave her my hand back, but she didn't take it. The sky darkened, and we still hadn't found each other. I met her that same evening in another hotel room, and when I was finally able to run my fingers through her hair, I started to live again.

'I … I loved making love with her.'

'The following afternoon, we met in the same spot, and the day after that … Then it was the day before Christmas Eve, we were going to part. I wanted to ask her what her plans were, but I couldn't seem to open my mouth. I was afraid – there was something in my gut that kept me from smiling at her.

'She was sitting on the bed. I came close to her and laid my head on her thigh.

' "What's going to become of us?" she asked.

'I didn't say a word.

' "Yesterday, when you left me here in this hotel room in the middle of the afternoon, I told myself that I would

114

never go through this again. Never again, do you hear? Never ... I got dressed, and I went out. I didn't know where to go. I don't want to do this again; I can't lie down with you in a hotel room and then have you walk out the door afterwards. It's too difficult."

'She had a hard time getting her words out.

' "I promised myself that I would never go through this again with a man who would make me suffer. I don't think I deserve it, do you understand? I don't deserve it. So that's why I'm asking you: What's going to become of us?"

'I stayed silent.

' "You have nothing to say? I thought so. What could you say, anyway? What could you possibly do? You have your wife and your kids. And me, what am I? I'm almost nothing in your life. I live so far away ... so far away and so strangely ... I don't know how to live like other people. No house, no furniture, no cat, no cookbooks, no plans. I thought I was the smart one, that I understood life better than other people. I was proud of myself for not falling into the trap. And then you came along, and I feel completely at sea.

' "And now I'd like to slow down a bit because I found out that life is wonderful with you. I told you I was going to try to live without you ... I tried and I tried, but I'm not that strong; I think about you all the time. So I'm asking you now and maybe for the last time: What do you plan to do with me?"

' "Love you."

' "What else?"

' "I promise that I will never leave you behind in a hotel room ever again. I promise you."

'And then I turned and put my head back between her thighs. She lifted me up by the hair.

' "And what else?"

' "I love you. I'm only happy when I'm with you. I love only you. I … I … Trust me …"

'She let go of my head and our conversation ended there. I took her tenderly, but she didn't let herself go, she just let it happen. It's not the same thing.'

'What happened after that?'

'After that we parted for the first time … I say "the first time" because we broke it off so many times … Then I called her … I begged her … I found an excuse to return to China. I saw her room, her landlady …

'I stayed for a week. While she was at work I played plumber, electrician, and mason. I worked like a fiend for Miss Li, who spent her time singing and playing with her birds. She showed me the port of Hong Kong and took me to visit an old English lady who thought I was Lord Mountbatten! I played the part, if you can imagine!'

'Can you understand what all this meant for me? For the little boy who had never dared to take the lift to the sixth floor? My entire life was spent between two arrondissements in Paris and a little country house. I never saw my parents happy, my only brother suffocated to death, and I married my first girlfriend, the sister of one of my friends, because I didn't know how to pull out in time …

'That was it. That was my life …

'Can you understand? I felt as though I had been born a second time, as though it had all started again, in her arms, on that dubious harbour, in that damp little room of Miss Li's …'

He stopped talking.

'Was that Christine?'

'No, it was before Christine … That one was a miscarriage.'

'I didn't know.'

'No one knows. What is there to know? I got married to a young girl whom I loved, but in the way that you love a young girl. A pure, romantic love; the first rush of feelings … The wedding was a pretty sad affair. It felt like my first communion all over again.

'Suzanne also hadn't imagined that things would happen so quickly. She lost her youth and her illusions in one fell swoop. We both lost everything, while her father got the perfect son-in-law. I had just graduated from the top engineering school and he couldn't imagine anything better, since his sons were studying … *literature*. He could barely pronounce the word.

'Suzanne and I were not madly in love, but we were kind to each other. At that time, the one made up for the other.

'I'm telling you all this, but I really don't know if you can fully understand. Things have changed so much … It was forty years ago, but it seems like two centuries. It was a time when girls got married when they missed their periods. This must seem prehistoric to you …'

He rubbed his face.

'So, where was I? Oh yes … I was saying that I found myself halfway around the world with a woman who earned her living jumping from one continent to another and who seemed to love me for who I was, for what was inside. A woman who loved me, I'm tempted to say … tenderly. All of this was very, very new. Very exotic. A marvellous woman who held her breath while watching me eat cobra soup with chrysanthemum flowers.'

'Was it good?'

'A bit gelatinous for my taste …'

He smiled.

'And when I got back on the plane, for the first time in my life I was not afraid. I said to myself: let it explode, let it fall out of the sky and crash, it doesn't matter.'

'Why did you tell yourself that?'

'Why?'

'Yes, why? I would have said just the opposite … I'd tell myself: "Now I know why I'm afraid, and this goddamn plane better not fall!" '

'Yes, you're right. That would have been smarter … But there you are, and this is the heart of the problem: I didn't say that. I was probably even hoping that it would crash … My life would have been so much simpler …'

'You had just met the woman of your life and you thought about dying?'

'I didn't say I wanted to die!'

'I didn't say that either. I said you *thought about* dying …'

'I probably think about dying every day, don't you?'

'No.'

…

'Do you think your life is worth something?'

'Uh … Yes … A little, anyway … And then there are the children …'

'That's a good reason.'

He had settled back down in the armchair and his face was once again hidden.

'Yes. I agree with you, it was absurd. But I had just been so happy, so happy … I was intrigued and also a bit terrified. Was it normal to be so happy? Was it right? What price was I going to have to pay for all that?

'Because … Was it because of my upbringing or what the priests told me? Was it in my character? I'm not always good at seeing things clearly, but one thing is sure: I've always compared myself to a workhorse. Bit, reins, blinkers, plough, yoke, cart, and furrow … the whole thing. Since I was a boy, I have walked in the street with my head down, staring at the ground as though it had a crust – hard earth to be broken up.

'Marriage, family, work, the maze of social life, everything. I have always worked with lowered head and clamped jaw. Dreading everything. Mistrustful. I'm very good at squash, or I used to be, and it's not by chance – I like the feeling of being shut up in a cramped room, whacking a ball as hard as possible so that it comes back at me like a cannonball. I really liked that.

' "You like squash and I like swingball, and that explains everything … " Mathilde said one evening as she was massaging my aching shoulder. She was quiet for a moment, then added, "You should think about what I just said, it's not that dumb. People who are rigid inside are always bumping into life and hurting themselves in the process, but people who are soft – no, not soft, *supple* is the word – yes, that's it, supple on the inside, well, when they take a hit they suffer less … I think that you should take up swingball, it's much more fun. You hit the ball and you don't know where it's going to come back, but you know it will come back because of the string, and it makes for a wonderful moment of suspense. But you see, for example, I sometimes think … that I'm your swingball …"

'I didn't react, and she kept rubbing me in silence.'

*

'You never thought about starting your life over again with her?'

'Of course I did. A thousand times.

'A thousand times I wanted to and a thousand times I gave it up ... I went right to the edge of the abyss, I leaned over, and then I fled. I felt accountable to Suzanne, to the children.

'Accountable for what? There's another difficult question ... I was committed. I had signed, I had promised, I had to fulfil my obligations. Adrien was sixteen, and nothing was going right. He changed schools all the time, scribbled *No Future* in English in the lift, and the only thing on his mind was to go to London and come back with a pet rat. Suzanne was distraught. Here was something stronger than her. Who had changed her little boy? For the first time, I watched her waver; she spent whole evenings without saying a word. I couldn't see myself making the situation worse. I told myself ... I told myself that ...'

'What did you tell yourself?'

'Wait a moment, it's so grotesque ... I have to find the words I used at the time ... I must have told myself something like: "I am an example for my children. Here they are, on the threshold of their adult lives, about to scale the wall, a time when they are thinking about making important decisions. What a horrendous example for them if I were to leave their mother now ..." Rather lofty sentiments, don't you think? "How will they face things afterwards? What sort of chaos would I be causing? What irreparable damage? I am not a perfect father, far from it, but I am still the most obvious role model for them, and the nearest, and therefore ... hmmm ... I must keep myself in check." '

He grimaced.

'Wasn't that good? You have to admit it was priceless, no?'

I said nothing.

'I was especially thinking of Adrien ... of being a model of commitment for my son, Adrien ... You have the right to snigger with me at that one, you know. Don't hold back. It's not often you get the chance to hear a good joke.'

I shook my head.

'And yet ... Oh, what's the use? That was all so long ago ... so very long ago ...'

'And yet what?'

'Well ... There was one moment when I came very close to the abyss ... Really very near ... I started looking around to buy a studio. I thought about taking Christine away for a weekend. I thought about what I would say; I rehearsed certain scenes in my car. I even made an appointment with my accountant, and then one morning – you see what a tease life can be – Françoise came into my office in tears ...'

'Françoise? Your secretary?'

'Yes.

'Her husband had just left her ... I didn't recognise her

any more. She was always so exuberant, so imperious, this little woman who was in control of both herself and the universe – I watched her waste away day after day. In tears, losing weight, stumbling about, suffering. She suffered terribly. She took pills, lost more weight, and took the first sick leave of her career. She cried. She even cried in front of me. And what did I do, upright man that I was? I screwed up my courage and ... went along with the crowd. *What a bastard*, I agreed, what a bastard. How could he do that to his wife? How could he be so selfish, to just close the door and wash his hands of the whole thing? Step out of his life like he was going for a walk? Why ... why, that was too easy! Too easy!

'No, really, what a bastard. What a bastard that man was! No, sir, I'm not like you! I'm not leaving my wife, sir. I'm not leaving my wife, and I despise you ... Yes, I despise you from the depths of my soul, sir!

'That's what I thought. I was only too happy to get out of it so easily. Only too happy to assuage my conscience and stroke my beard. Oh yes, I supported my Françoise, I spoiled her. Oh yes, I often agreed. Oh no, I kept repeating to her, what bad luck you've had. What bad luck ...

'In fact, I secretly had to thank him, this Mr Jarmet whom I didn't know from Adam. I was secretly grateful to him. He handed me the solution on a silver platter. Thanks to him, thanks to his disgraceful behaviour, I could return to my comfortable little situation with my head held high. Work, Family, and Country, that was me. Head high and walking tall! I prided myself on it, as you can imagine, you know me … I had arrived at the agreeable conclusion that … I wasn't like other people. I was a notch above them. Not much, but above. I wouldn't leave my wife, no, not me …'

'Was that when you broke it off with Mathilde?'

'What on earth for? No, not in the least. I continued to see her, but I shelved my escape plans and stopped wasting time looking at horrible little studios. Because you see, as I have just brilliantly demonstrated, that's not the stuff I was made of: I wasn't about to stir up a hornet's nest. That was for irresponsible types, all that. For a husband who cheats with his secretary.'

His voice was filled with sarcasm, and he was trembling with rage.

'No, I didn't break it off with her, I continued to tenderly screw her, promising things like *always* and *later*.'

'Really?'

'Yes.'

'You mean like in all those trashy stories?'

'Yes.'

'You asked her to be patient, and promised her all kinds of things?'

'Yes.'

'How did she stand it?'

'I don't know, really. I don't know …'

'Maybe because she loved you?'

'Perhaps.'

He drained his glass.

'Perhaps, yes … Maybe she did …'

'And you didn't leave because of Françoise?'

'Exactly. Because of Jean-Paul Jarmet, to be precise. Well, that's what I say now, but if it hadn't been him, I would have found some other excuse. Two-faced people are good at finding excuses. Very good.'

'It's incredible …'

'What is?'

'This story … To see what it hinges on. It's incredible.'

'No, my dear Chloé, it's not incredible … it's not incredible at all. It's life. It's what life is like for nearly everyone. We hedge, we make arrangements, we keep our cowardice close to us, like a pet. *C'est la vie.* There are those who are courageous and those who settle, and it's so much less tiring to settle … Pass me that bottle.'

'Are you going to get drunk?'

'No, I'm not going to get drunk. I've never been able to. The more I drink, the more lucid I become …'

'How awful!'

'As you say, how awful … Can I offer you some?'

'No, thanks.'

'Would you like that herbal tea now?'

'No, no. I'm … I don't know what I am … dumbstruck, maybe.'

'Dumbstruck by what?'

'By you, of course! I've never heard you speak more than two sentences at once, you never raise your voice, you never make a scene. Not once, since the first time I saw you play the Grand Inquisitor. I never caught you in the act of being tender or sensitive, and now, all of a sudden, you dump all of this on me without even yelling *Timber! ...*'

'Do you find it shocking?'

'No, not at all! That's not it! On the contrary ... On the contrary ... But ... But how have you managed to play that role all this time?'

'What role?'

'That one ... the role of the old bastard.'

'But, Chloé, I am an old bastard! I'm an old bastard – this is what I've been trying to explain to you this whole time!'

'But no! If you're aware of it, it's because you aren't one after all. The real ones aren't aware of anything!'

'Psshhh, don't believe that one ... It's just another one of my tricks to get out of this honourably. I'm very talented that way ...'

He smiled at me.

'It's incredible, just incredible.'

'What?'

'All of this. Everything you've told me.'

'No, it's not incredible. On the contrary, it's all quite banal.

'Very, very banal ... I'm telling you because it's you, because it's here, in this room, in this house, because it's night, and because Adrien has made you suffer. Because his choice makes me feel both hopeless and reassured.

Because I don't like to see you unhappy. I've caused too much suffering myself ... And because I would rather see you suffer a lot today than suffer a little bit for the rest of your life.

'I see people suffering a little, only a little, not much at all, just enough to ruin their lives completely ... Yes, at my age, I see that a great deal ... People who are still together because they're crushed under the weight of that miserable little thing – their ordinary little life. All those compromises, all of those contradictions ... All of that to end up ...

'Bravo! Hurray! We've managed to bury it all: our friends, our dreams, our loves, and now, now it's our turn! Bravo, my friends, bravo!'

He applauded.

'Retirees, they call them. Retired from everything. How I hate them. I hate them, do you hear me? I hate them because I see myself in them. There they are, wallowing in self-satisfaction. *We made it, we made it!* they seem to say, without ever really having been there for each other. But my God, at what price? What price?! Regrets, remorse, cracks and compromises that don't heal over, that never heal. Never! Not even in the Hesperides. Not even posing for the photo with the great-grandchildren. Not even when you both answer the game-show question at the exact same moment.'

He said he'd never been drunk before, but ...

He stopped talking and gesticulating. We sat like that for a long moment. In silence. Except for the muted fireworks in the chimney.

...

'I didn't finish telling you about Françoise ...'

He had calmed down, and I had to strain my ears to hear him.

'A few years ago, it was in '94, I think, she became seriously ill ... Very seriously ... A goddamn cancer that was eating away at her abdomen. They started by removing one ovary, then the other, then her uterus ... I don't know much about it, really; she never confided in me, as you can imagine, but it turned out to be much more serious than they had imagined. Françoise was calculating the time she had left. She wanted to make it to Christmas. Easter was too much to hope for.

'One day, I called her at the hospital and offered to lay her off with a huge severance package so that she could travel around the world when she got out, so she could go shopping at the top designers, pick out the prettiest dresses, and then sashay along the deck of a huge ocean liner sipping Pimm's. Françoise adored Pimm's ...

' "Save your money, I'll drink it with the others at your retirement party!"

'We chatted. We were good actors – we had a lump

in our throats but our exchange was upbeat. The latest prognosis was a disaster. I heard it from her daughter. Christmas looked doubtful.

' "Don't believe everything you hear, you're still not going to get your chance to replace me with some young thing," she chided me in a whisper before hanging up. I pretended to grumble and found myself in tears in the middle of the afternoon. I found out how much I cared for her as well. How much I needed her. Seventeen years we had worked together. Always, every day. Seventeen years she put up with me, helped me ... She knew about Mathilde and never said a word. Not to me, nor to anyone else. She smiled at me when I was unhappy, and shrugged her shoulders when I was disagreeable. She was barely twenty years old when she came to work for me. She didn't know how to do anything. She was a graduate of a hotel school, and quit a job because a cook had pinched her bottom. She told me this during our first meeting. She didn't want anyone pinching her bottom, and she didn't want to go back to live with her parents in the Creuse. She would only go back when she had her own car, so she could be sure that she could leave! I hired her because of that sentence.

'She, too, was my princess.'

'I called from time to time to complain about her substitute.

'And then, a long time afterwards, I went to see her, when she finally let me. It was in the spring. She had changed hospitals. The treatment was less aggressive and her progress had encouraged her doctors, who stopped by to congratulate her on being good-natured and a real fighter. On the phone, she told me she had started to give advice about everything and to everyone. She had ideas for changing the décor, and she had started a quilting circle. She criticised their foul-ups and poor organisation. She asked to meet with someone from social services to clear up a few simple problems. I teased her, and she defended herself: "But it's common sense! Just good common sense, you see!" She was back in fighting form, and I drove to the clinic with a happy heart.

'And yet, seeing her again was a shock. She was no longer my princess; in her place was a jaundiced little bird. Her neck, her cheeks, her hands, her arms – everything had disappeared. Her skin was yellowish and somewhat coarse, and her eyes had doubled in size. What shocked me the most was her wig. She had probably put it on in a hurry, and the parting wasn't quite in the middle. I tried to fill her in on the news from the office, about Caroline's baby and the contracts under way, but I was obsessed by that wig. I was afraid it was going to slip.

'At that moment, a man knocked on the door. "Oops!" he said when he saw me before turning around. Françoise called him back. "Pierre, this is Simon, my friend. I don't believe you two have ever met ..." I got up. No, we had never met. I didn't even know he existed. We were so discreet, Françoise and I ... He shook my hand very firmly and there was all the kindness in the world in his eyes. Two little grey eyes, intelligent, alive, and tender. While I sat back down, he went over to Françoise to kiss her, and then do you know what he did?'

'No.'

'He took that little broken doll's face in his hands as if he wanted to kiss her enthusiastically, and he took advantage of that to straighten her wig. She cursed and told him to be careful, I was her boss after all, and he laughed before he went out, on the pretext of wanting to get the paper.

'And when he had closed the door, Françoise slowly turned towards me. Her eyes were full of tears. She murmured, "Without him, I would have come to the end by now, you know … If I'm putting up a fight, it's because there is so much I want to do with him. So many things …"

'Her smile was frightful. Her jaw was huge, almost indecent. I had the feeling that her teeth were going to come out. That the skin on her cheeks would split. I was overcome with nausea. And the smell … That smell of drugs and death and Guerlain perfume all mixed together. I could barely stand it, and I had to fight to keep from putting my hand over my mouth. I thought I was going to lose it. My vision blurred. It was hardly noticeable, you know, I pretended to pinch my nose and rub my eyes as if I had a speck of dust in them. When I looked up at her again, forcing myself to smile, she asked, "Are you all right?" "Yes, yes, I'm fine," I answered. I could feel my mouth curving into a sad child's frown. "I'm fine, it's fine … It's just that … I don't think you look all that well, Françoise …" She closed her eyes and laid her head on her pillow. "Don't you worry about me. I'm going to beat this … He needs me too much, that one does …" '

'I left completely broken up. I held myself up on the walls. I took forever to remember where I had parked my car, and I got lost in the damn parking garage. What was happening to me? My God, what was happening to me? Was it seeing her like that? Was it the smell of disinfected death, or just the place itself? That pall of misery, of suffering. And my little Françoise with her ravaged arms, my angel lost in the midst of all those zombies. Lost in her minuscule bed. What had they done to my princess? Why had they mistreated her like that?

'It took forever to find my car and forever to get it started, then it took me several minutes to put it in first gear. And you know what? Do you know why I was reeling like that? It wasn't because of her, or her catheters, or her suffering. Of course it wasn't. It was …'

He lifted his head.

'It was despair. Yes, the boomerang had come back to hit me in the face …'

*

Silence.

...

I finally said:

'Pierre?'

'Yes?'

'You're going to think I'm kidding, but I think I'll have herbal tea now ...'

He got up, complaining in order to hide his gratitude.

'Oh, you women never know what you want; you can be so annoying ...'

I followed him into the kitchen and sat down on the other side of the table, while he put a pan of water on the burner. The light from the suspension lamp was harsh. I pulled it down as far as it would go while he rummaged through all the cupboards.

'Can I ask you a question?'

'If you can tell me where to find what I'm looking for.'

'Right there, in front of you, in that red box.'

'That one? We never used to put it there, it seems to me that – Oh sorry, I'm listening.'

'How many years were you together?'

'With Mathilde?'

'Yes.'

'Between Hong Kong and our final discussion, five years and seven months.'

'And did you spend a lot of time together?'

'No, I already told you. A few hours, a few days …'

'And was that enough?'

He said nothing.

'Was it enough for you?'

'No, of course not. Well, yes really, since I never did anything to change the situation. It's what I told myself afterwards. Maybe it suited me. "Suited" – what an ugly word that is. Perhaps it suited me to have a reassuring wife on one side and a thrill on the other. Dinner on the table every night and the feeling that I could sneak off from time to time … A full stomach and all the comforts of home. It was practical, and comfortable.'

'You called her when you needed her?'

'Yes, that was more or less the case …'

He set a mug down in front of me.

'Well, no, actually … It didn't happen exactly like that … One day, right at the beginning, she wrote me a letter. The only one she ever sent, by the way. It read:

'I've thought about it, I don't have any illusions, I love you but I don't trust you. Because what we are living is not real, it's a game. And because it's a game, we have to have rules. I don't want to see you in Paris. Not in Paris or in any other place that makes you afraid. When I'm with you, I want to hold your hand in the street and kiss you in restaurants, otherwise I'm not interested. I'm too old to play cat and mouse. Therefore, we will see each other as far away as possible, in other countries. When you know where you will be, you will write to me at this address, it's my sister's in London, she'll know where to forward it. Don't take the trouble to write a love letter, just the details. Tell me which hotel you're in and when and where. If I can join you, I'll come, otherwise too bad. Don't try to call me, or to find out where I am or how I'm living, this is no longer the issue. I've thought it over, I think it's the best solution: to do the same as you, live my own life, and be fond of you from a distance. I don't want to wait for your phone calls, I don't want to keep myself from falling in love, I want to be able to sleep with whom

135

I want, when I want, and with no scruples. Because you're right, a life without scruples is more ... *convenient*. That's not the way I see things, but why not? I'll give it a try. What do I have to lose, after all? A cowardly man? And what do I stand to gain? The pleasure of sleeping in your arms sometimes ... I've thought about it, I want to give it a try. Take it or leave it ...

'What is it?'

'Nothing. It's amusing to see that you had found an opponent equal to you.'

'No, unfortunately I hadn't. She went through the motions and acted like a femme fatale, but she was really soft-hearted. I didn't know it when I accepted her proposal, I only found out much later. Five years and seven months later ...

'Actually, that's a lie. I read between the lines, I guessed what those sorts of phrases must have cost her. But I wasn't going to dwell on it, because these rules suited me fine. They suited me down to the ground. All I had to do was step up the import-export department and get used to take-offs, and that was that. A letter like that is a godsend for men who want to cheat on their wives without complications. Of course, I was bothered by all that talk about sleeping around and falling in love, but we weren't at that point yet ...'

He sat down at the end of the table, at his usual place.

'Pretty smart of me, eh? Oh, I was a smart one then ...

Especially because the whole thing helped me make a lot of money ... I had always neglected the international side of the business a bit ...'

'Why all the cynicism?'

'You gave a very good answer to that question yourself a little while ago ...'

I leaned down to get the tea strainer.

'In addition, it was very romantic ... I would get off the plane, my heart pounding, I checked into the hotel hoping that my key wouldn't be on its hook, I put my bags down in strange rooms, rummaging around to see if she had already been there, I went off to work, I came back in the evening praying to God she would be in my bed. Sometimes she was, sometimes not. She would join me in the middle of the night and we would lose ourselves in each other without exchanging a single word. We laughed under the covers, amazed to find each other there. At last. So far away, and so close. Sometimes, she would only arrive the next day, and I spent the night sitting at the bar, and listening for noises in the corridor. Sometimes she took another room, ordering me to come and join her in the early morning hours. Sometimes she didn't show and I hated her. I would return to Paris in a very bad mood. At first, I really had work to do; later, I had less and less ... I made up any excuse to be able to leave. Sometimes I saw something of the country, and sometimes I saw nothing but my hotel room. Sometimes we never even left the airport. It was ridiculous. There was no logic to it. Sometimes we would talk nonstop, and other times we had nothing to say to each other. True to her word, Mathilde never talked about her love life, or only during pillow talk. She talked about men and situations that drove me wild, but that was only between the sheets … I was completely at the mercy of that woman, of the mischievous little way she had of pretending to say the wrong name in the dark. I acted annoyed, but I was devastated. I took her even more forcefully, when all I wanted to do was hold her tightly in my arms.

'When one of us joked, the other one suffered. It was completely absurd. I dreamed of catching hold of her and shaking her until all her venom was gone. Until she told me she loved me. Until she told me she loved me, damn it all. But I couldn't, it was me that was the bastard. All of this was my fault …'

He got up to find his glass.

'What was I thinking? That it was going to go on like that for years? For years on end? No, I didn't believe that. We would say goodbye to each other furtively, sadly, awkwardly, without ever talking about the next time. No, it was untenable … And the more I hesitated, the more I loved her, and the more I loved her, the less I believed it. I felt overwhelmed, powerless, caught in my own web. Immobile and resigned.'

'Resigned to what?'

'To losing her one day …'

'I don't understand.'

'Oh yes, you do. You understand what I'm saying … What could I have possibly done? Answer me that.'

'I can't.'

'No, of course you can't answer … You're the last person in the world who could answer that question.'

'What exactly did you promise her?'

'I don't remember now … not much, I imagine, or else the unimaginable. No, not very much … I had the decency to shut my eyes when she asked me questions, and to kiss her when she waited for me to answer. I was almost fifty and I thought I was old. I thought this was the end of the road, a bright, happy ending … I said to myself: "Don't rush into things, she's so young, she'll be the first to leave." And every time I saw her again, I was amazed but also surprised. What? She's still here? But why? I had a hard time seeing what she liked in me, and I told myself, "Why get into a mess, since she's going to leave me?" It was inevitable, it was sure to happen. There was no reason for her to still be there the next time, no reason at all … In the end, I was practically hoping that she wouldn't be there. Up to then, life had been so kind as to decide everything for me, why should that change now? Why? I had proved that I didn't have the ability to take things in hand … Business, yes, that was a game and I was the best, but on the home front? I preferred to suffer; I wanted to console myself by thinking that I was the one who was suffering. I wanted to dream or regret. It's so much simpler that way ...

'My great-aunt on my father's side was Russian, and she used to tell me:

' "You, you're like my father, you have nostalgia for the mountains."

' "Which mountains, Mouschka?" I would ask.

' "Why, the ones you've never seen, of course!" '

'She told you that?'

'Yes. She said it each time I looked out the window ...'

'And what were you looking at?'

'The bus depot!'

He laughed.

'Another character you would have liked ... Some Friday I'll tell you about her.'

'We'll go to Chez Dominique, then ...'

'As I told you, wherever and whenever you want to go.'

He filled my mug with tea.

'But what was she doing all that time?'

'I don't know ... She was working. She had found a job at UNESCO, but had left it shortly after. She didn't like translating their smooth talk. She couldn't stand being cooped up day after day, mindlessly repeating politicians' rhetoric. She preferred the business world, where the adrenaline was of a higher calibre. She travelled around, went to visit her brothers, sisters, and friends who were scattered all over the globe. She lived in Norway for a time, but she didn't like it there either, with all those blue-eyed ayatollahs, and where she was always cold ... And when she had enough of jet lag, she stayed in London translating technical manuals. She loved her nephews.'

'But aside from work?'

'Ah, that ... that is shrouded in mystery. God knows I tried to drag it out of her ... She closed up, hesitated, wriggled out of my questions. "At least leave me that," she said. "Let me keep my dignity. The dignity of those who are discreet. Is that too much to ask?" Or she would give me a taste of my own medicine and torture me, laughing all the while. "In fact, didn't I tell you I got married last month? How stupid of me, I wanted to show you the pictures but I forgot them. His name is Billy; he's not very smart but he takes good care of me ..." '

'Did that make you laugh?'

'No, not really.'

'You loved her?'

'Yes.'

'Loved her how?'

'I loved her.'

'And what do you remember from those years?'

'A life like a dotted line ... Nothing, then something. Then nothing again. And then something. Then nothing again ... It went by very quickly ... When I think about it, it seems like the whole thing only lasted a season ... Not even a season, the length of a single breath. A sort of mirage ... We had no daily life together. That was what

Mathilde suffered from the most, I think ... I suspected it, mind you, but the proof came one evening after a long day of work.

'When I came in, she was sitting at a small desk, writing something on the hotel stationery. She had already filled a dozen pages with her small, cramped handwriting.

' "Who are you writing to like that?" I asked her, bending over her neck.

' "To you." '

' "Me?" '

'*She's leaving me*, I thought, and at once I began to feel ill.

' "What is it? You're completely pale. Are you all right?"

' "Why are you writing to me?"

' "Oh, I'm not really writing you a letter, I'm writing down all the things I want to do with you ..."

'There were pages everywhere. Around her, at her feet, on the bed. I picked one up at random:

'... go for a picnic, have a nap on the bank of a river, eat peaches, shrimps, croissants, sticky rice, swim, dance, buy myself shoes, lingerie, perfume, read the paper, window-shop, take the Métro, watch time pass, push you over when you're taking up all the room, hang out the laundry, go to the opera, to Bayreuth, to Vienna, to the races, to the supermarket, have a barbecue, complain because you forgot the charcoal, brush my teeth at the same time as you, buy you underwear, cut the grass, read the paper over your shoulder, keep you from eating too many peanuts, visit the vineyards in the Loire, and those in Hunter Valley, act like an idiot, talk my head off, introduce you to Martha and Tino, pick blackberries, cook, go back to Vietnam, wear a sari, garden, wake you up because you're snoring again, go to the zoo, to the flea market, to Paris, to London, to Melrose, to Piccadilly, sing you songs, stop smoking, ask you to trim my nails, buy dishes, foolish things, things that have no purpose, eat ice cream, people-watch, beat you at chess, listen to jazz, reggae, dance the mambo and the cha-cha, get bored, throw tantrums, pout, laugh, wrap you around my little finger, look for a house among the cows, fill up huge shopping trolleys, repaint a ceiling, sew curtains, spend hours around a table talking with interesting people, grab you by the goatee, cut your hair, pull up weeds, wash the car, see the sea, watch old B-movies, call you up again, say dirty words to you, learn to knit, knit you a scarf, unravel that horrible scarf, collect cats, dogs, parrots, elephants, rent bicycles, not use them, stay in a hammock, reread my grandmother's *Winnie Winkle* adventures, look at Winnie's dresses again, drink margaritas in the shade, cheat, learn to use an iron, throw the iron out of the window, sing in the rain, run away from tourists, get drunk, tell you everything, remember that some things are better left unsaid, listen to you, give you my hand, go and find the iron, listen to the words of songs, set the alarm, forget our suitcases, stop rushing off everywhere, put out the trash, ask you if you still love me, chat with the neighbour, tell you about my childhood in Bahrain, my nanny's rings, the smell of henna and balls of amber, make toast for eggs, labels for jam jars …

'It went on like that for pages. Page after page … I'm just telling you the ones that come into my head, the ones I remember. It was incredible.

' "How long have you been writing that?"

' "Since you left."

' "But why?"

' "Because I'm bored," she answered cheerfully. "I'm dying of boredom, if you can believe it!" '

'I picked up the whole stack and sat down on the edge of the bed to see better. I was smiling but, to tell you the truth, I was paralysed by so much desire, so much energy. But I smiled anyway. She had a way of putting things that was so amusing, so witty, and she was watching my reactions. On one page, between "start from scratch" and "paste pictures in a photo album" she had written "a baby". Just like that, with no commentary. I continued to examine this huge list without batting an eyelid while she bit her cheeks.

' "Well?" She wasn't breathing any more. "What do you think?"

' "Who are Martha and Tino?" I asked her.

'From the shape of her mouth, the way her shoulders slumped, how her hand dropped, I knew that I was going to lose her. Just by asking that stupid question, I had put my head on the block. She went into the bathroom and said, "Some nice people," before shutting the door. And instead of going to her, instead of throwing myself at her feet saying yes, anything she wanted because yes, I was put on this earth to make her happy, I went out on the balcony to smoke a cigarette.'

'And then?'

'And then nothing. The cigarette tasted terrible. We went down to dinner. Mathilde was beautiful. More beautiful than ever, it seemed to me. Lively, vivacious. Everyone looked at her. The women turned their heads and the men smiled at me. She was ... how shall I say it ... she was radiant ... Her skin, her face, her smile, her hair, her gestures, everything in her captured the light and gracefully reflected it back. It was a mixture of vitality and tenderness that never ceased to amaze me. "You're beautiful," I told her. She shrugged. "In your eyes." "Yes," I agreed, "in my eyes ..."

'When I think about her today, after all these years, that's the first image that comes to mind – her long neck, her dark eyes, and her little brown dress in that Austrian dining room, shrugging her shoulders.'

'After all, it was intentional, all of that beauty and grace. She knew very well what she was doing that evening: she was making herself unforgettable. Perhaps I'm mistaken, but I don't think so ... It was her swan song, her farewell, her white handkerchief waving at the window. She was so perceptive, she must have known it ... Even her skin was softer. Was she aware of it? Was she being generous or simply cruel? Both, I think ... It was both ...

'And that night, after the caresses and the sighing, she said:

' "Can I ask you a question?"

' "Yes."

' "Will you give me an answer?"

' "Yes."

'I opened my eyes.

' "Don't you think that we go well together?"

'I was disappointed; I was expecting a question a bit more ... um ... provocative.

' "Yes."

' "Do you think so, too?"

' "Yes."

' "I think we go well together ... I like being with you because I'm never bored. Even when we're not talking, even when we're not touching, even when we're not in the same room, I'm not bored. I'm never bored. I think it's because I have confidence in you, in your thoughts. Do you understand? I love everything I see in you, and everything I don't see. I know your faults, but as it turns out, I feel as though your faults go well with my qualities. We're not afraid of the same things. Even our inner demons go well together! You, you're worth more than you show, and I'm just the opposite. I need your gaze in order to have a bit more ... a bit more substance? What is the word?" Her French failed her. "Complexity? When you want to say that someone is interesting inside?"

' "Depth?" '

' "That's it! I'm like a kite; unless someone holds me by the string, I fly away … And you, it's funny … I often say to myself that you are strong enough to hold me and smart enough to let me go …" '

' "Why are you telling me all this?" '

' "Because I want you to know." '

' "Why now?" '

' "I don't know … Perhaps it's because it's incredible to meet someone and say: with this person, I'm happy." '

' "But why are you saying this to me now?" '

' "Because sometimes I have the feeling that you don't understand how lucky we are …" '

' "Mathilde?" '

' "Yes?" '

' "Are you going to leave me?" '

' "No." '

' "You're not happy?" '

' "Not very." '

'And then we stopped talking.'

'The next day we went tramping around the mountains, and the day after, we each went our separate ways.'

•••

My tea was getting cold.

'Was that the end?'

147

'Nearly.'

*

'A few weeks later, she came to Paris and asked if I could spare her a few moments. I was both happy and annoyed. We walked for a long time, barely speaking, and then I took her to lunch on the Champs-Elysées.

'While I was getting up the courage to take her hands in mine, she stunned me by saying:

' "Pierre, I'm pregnant."

' "By whom?" I answered, growing pale.

'She rose to her feet, radiant.

' "No one."

'She put on her coat and pushed the chair back in place. There was a magnificent smile on her face.

' "Thank you, you said the words that I was expecting. I came all this way to hear you say those two words. I took a bit of a risk."

'I stuttered; I wanted to get up, but the table leg was … She made a gesture:

' "Don't move."

'Her eyes shone.

' "I got what I wanted. I couldn't bring myself to leave you. I can't spend my life waiting for you, but I … Nothing. I needed to hear those two words. I needed to see your cowardice. To experience it up close, do you understand? No, don't move … Don't move, I tell you! Don't move! I have to go now. I'm so tired … If only you knew how tired I was, Pierre … I … I can't do this any more …"

'I stood up.

' "You are going to let me leave, right? You are going to let me? You have to let me leave now, you have to let me …" Her voice caught. "You're going to let me leave, aren't you?"

'I nodded.

' "But you know I love you, you know that, don't you?" I finally managed to say.

'She moved away and turned back before opening the door. She looked at me intently and shook her head from left to right.'

...

My father-in-law got up to kill an insect on the lamp.

He emptied the last of the bottle into his glass.

'And that was the end?'

'Yes.'

'You didn't go after her?'

'Like in the movies?'

'Yes. In slow motion …'

'No. I went to bed.'

'You went to bed?'

'Yes.'

'But where?'

'At home, of course!'

'Why?'

'A great weakness, a great, great weariness ... For several months, I had been obsessed by the image of a dead tree. At all times of the day and night, I dreamed I was climbing a dead tree and that I let myself slide down its hollow trunk. The fall was so gentle, so gentle ... as if I were bouncing on the top of a parachute. I would bounce, fall farther, and then bounce again. I thought about it constantly. In meetings, at the dinner table, in my car, while I was trying to sleep. I climbed my tree and let myself fall.'

'Was it depression?'

'Don't use such a big word, please, no big words ... You know how it is at the Dippels'.' He chuckled. 'You said so a while ago. No moodiness, no bile, no spleen. No, I couldn't allow myself to give in to that kind of whim. So I came down with hepatitis. It was more convenient. I woke up the next day and the whites of my eyes were lemon yellow. Everything tasted bad, my urine was dark, and the deed was done. A vicious case of hepatitis for someone who travelled a good deal, it was patently obvious.

'Christine undressed me that day.

'I couldn't move ... For a month I stayed in bed, nauseous and exhausted. When I was thirsty, I waited until someone came in and held out a glass, and when I was cold, I didn't have the strength to pull up the coverlet. I no longer spoke. I forbade people to open the shutters. I had become an old man. Everything exhausted me: Suzanne's kindness, my powerlessness, the whispering of the children. Could someone please close the door once and for all and leave me alone with my sorrow? Would Mathilde have come if … Would she … Oh … I was so tired. And all of my memories, my regrets, and my cowardice just knocked me down even more. With half-closed eyes and stomach churning, I thought about the disaster my life had been. Happiness had been mine, and I had let it slip away in order to not complicate my life. And yet it was so simple. All I had to do was hold out my hand. The rest could have been settled one way or another. Everything falls into place when you're happy, don't you think?'

'I don't know.'

'But I know. Believe me, Chloé. I don't know much, but I know this. I'm not more psychic than the next person, but I'm twice your age. Twice your age, do you realise that? Life is stronger than you are, even when you deny it, even when you neglect it, even when you refuse to admit it. Stronger than anything. People came home from the camps and had children. Men and women who had been tortured, who had watched their loved ones die and their houses burn to the ground. They came home and ran for the bus, talked about the weather, and married their daughters off. It's incredible, but that's the way it is. Life is stronger than anything. And who are we to be so self-important? We bustle about, talk in loud voices, and for what? And then what happens, afterwards?

'What happened to little Sylvie, for whom Paul died in

the next room? What happened to her?

'The fire is going out.'

He got up to put another log on.

*

And me, I thought, where do I fit into all of this?

Where am I?

He crouched in front of the fireplace.

'Do you believe me, Chloé? Do you believe me when I say that life is stronger than you?'

'Certainly …'

'Do you trust me?'

'That depends on the day.'

'What about today?'

'Yes.'

'Then I think that you should go to bed now.'

'You never saw her again? You never tried to find out how she was? Never called her?'

He sighed.

'Haven't you had enough?'

'No.'

'I called her sister, of course, I even went there in person, but it didn't do any good. She had flown the coop … To find her, I had to know in which hemisphere to start looking … And then, I had promised I would leave her alone. That's one of my outstanding qualities, by the way. I'm a good loser.'

'What you're saying is completely ridiculous. It's not

about being a good or bad loser. That's completely stupid reasoning, stupid and childish. It wasn't a game, after all ... or was it? Was it all a game?'

He was delighted.

'Really, I don't have to worry about you, my girl. You have no idea how much I respect you. You are everything that I'm not, you are my star and your good sense will save us all ...'

'You're drunk, is that it?'

'You want to know something? I've never felt so good in my life!'

He lifted himself to his feet by holding on to the mantelpiece.

'Let's go to bed.'

'You haven't finished ...'

'You want to hear me ramble on some more?'

'Yes.'

'Why?'

'Because I love a good story.'

'You think that this is a good story?'

'Yes.'

'Me too ...'

'You saw her again, right? At the Palais-Royal?'

'How did you know that?'

'You told me yourself!'

'Oh really? Did I say that?'

I nodded.

'Well, then, this will be the last act …

'That day, I invited a group of clients to the Grand Véfour. Françoise had organised everything. Good vintages, flattery, excellent dishes. I pulled out all the stops. I had been doing the same thing forever, it seems … The lunch was utterly boring. I've always hated that sort of thing, spending hours at the table with men I don't give a damn for, being forced to listen to them go on about their work … And in addition, I was the killjoy of the group because of my liver. For a long time, I didn't drink a drop of alcohol and asked the waiters to tell me exactly what was in each dish. You know the type of pain in the arse I mean … Plus, I don't really care for the company of men. They bore me. They're the same as they were at boarding school. The braggarts are the same, and so are the brownnosers …'

'So, there I was at that point in my life, in front of the door of a fancy restaurant, a bit sluggish, a little weary, tapping another big cigar, dreaming of the moment when I could loosen my belt, when I caught sight of her. She was walking fast, almost running, and dragging a small, unhappy boy behind her. "Mathilde?" I murmured. I saw her turn pale, and the ground open under her feet. She didn't slow down. "Mathilde!" I said more loudly. "Mathilde!" And then I ran after her like a crazy thing. "Mathiiilde!" I nearly shouted. The little boy turned round.'

'I invited her for a coffee under the arcades. She didn't have the strength to refuse; she … She was still so beautiful. I tried to act naturally. I was a bit awkward, a bit stupid, a bit too playful. It was difficult.

'Where was she living? What was she doing here? I wanted her to tell me about herself. Tell me how you are. Do you live here? Do you live in Paris? She answered grudgingly. She was ill at ease and gnawed the end of her coffee spoon. At any rate, I wasn't listening, I had stopped listening. I was looking at this little blond boy who had collected all the leftover bread from nearby tables and was throwing crumbs to the birds. He had made two piles, one for the sparrows and one for the pigeons, and was busily organising this little world. The pigeons were not supposed to take the crumbs from the smaller birds. "*Go away, you!*" he yelled in English, giving them a kick. "Go away, you stupid bird!" When I turned back towards his mother, about to speak, she cut me short:

' "Don't bother, Pierre, don't bother. He's not five years old … He hasn't turned five, do you understand?"

'I closed my mouth.

' "What's his name?"

' "Tom."

' "He speaks English?"

' "English and French."

' "Do you have other children?"

' "No."

' "Do you … Are you … I mean … do you live with someone?"

'She scraped at the sugar in the bottom of her cup and smiled at me.

' "I have to go now. We're expected."

' "Already?"

'She stood up.

' "Can I drop you somewhere? I …"

'She picked up her bag.

' "Pierre, please …"

'And then, I broke down. I didn't expect it at all. I began to cry like a baby. I … That child was for me. It was for me to show him how to chase pigeons, for me to pick up his sweater and put his hat on. It was for me to do that. What's more, I knew she was lying! The boy was more than four. I wasn't blind after all! Why was she lying to me that way? Why had she lied to me? No one has the right to lie like that! No one … I sobbed. I wanted to say that –

'She pushed back her chair.

' "I'm going now. I've already cried all my tears." '

'And afterwards?'

'Afterwards I left …'

'No, I mean with Mathilde, what happened?'

'After that it was over.'

'Really over?'

'Over.'

There was a long silence.

'Was she lying?'

'No. Since then I started paying more attention. I compared him with other children, with your daughters … no, I think that she wasn't lying. Children are so big these days … With all the vitamins you put in their bottles … I think about him sometimes. He must be around fifteen today … He must be huge, that boy.'

'You never tried to see her again?'

'No.'

'What about now? Maybe she –'

'Now it's finished. Now I … I don't even know if I would still be capable of …'

He folded the fire screen.

'I don't want to talk about it any more.'

He went to lock the front door and turned out all the lights.

I hadn't moved from the couch.

'Come on, Chloé … Do you see what time it is? Go to bed now.'

I didn't answer.

'Do you hear me?'

'So love is just bullshit? That's it? It never works out?'

'Of course it works out. But you have to fight …'

'Fight how?'

'Every day you have to fight a bit. A little bit each day, with the courage to be yourself, to decide to be happ—'

'Oh, that's beautiful! You sound just like Paulo Coelho …'

'Go ahead and laugh, go ahead …'

'Being yourself, does that mean walking out on your wife and kids?'

'Who said anything about walking out on the kids?'

'Oh, stop it. You know exactly what I mean …'

'No, I don't.'

I started to cry again.

'Go on, leave. Leave me alone. I can't take any more of your noble sentiments. I can't take them any more. It's too much for me, Mr Bare-Your-Soul, it's too much …'

'I'm going, I'm going. Since you ask so nicely …'

At the door of the room, he said:

'One last story, if I may?'

I didn't want to hear it.

'One day, a long time ago, I took my little daughter to the bakery. It was rare for me to go to the bakery with my daughter. It was rare for us to hold hands, and even rarer to be alone with her. It must have been a Sunday morning, and the bakery was full of people buying fruit tarts and meringues. On the way out, she asked me for the tip of the baguette to eat. I refused. *No*, I said. *When we're at*

158

the table. We went home and sat down to eat. A perfect little family. I was the one who cut the bread. I insisted. I wanted to keep my promise. But when I handed the bread end to my daughter, she gave it to her brother.

' "But you told me you wanted it …"

' "I wanted it back then," she said, unfolding her napkin.

' "But it tastes the same," I insisted. "It's the same …"

'She turned away.

' "No thank you." '

'I'm going to bed, and I'll leave you in the dark if that's what you want, but before I turn out the lights, I want to ask one question. I'm not asking you, I'm not asking myself, I'm asking the walls:

'Wouldn't that stubborn little girl have preferred living with a father who was happier?'

Also by Anna Gavalda

Breaking Away

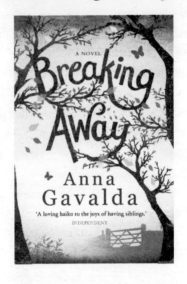

ISBN 9781908313614

£7.99